Illustrations by Grigory Kornienko
Publisher: BoD – Books on Demand, Stockholm, Sweden
Print: BoD – Books on Demand, Norderstedt, Germany
ISBN: 978-91-7969-658-0

# *Reaper's origins I*
# *Hellfire: Ignited*

This story takes place in a world where two powerful clans. The Demon Empire, with The Demon Emperor as their leader, and The Divine Kingdom, with The Divine King as their leader, were engaged in a raging war against each other.

This caused a rain of pain, destruction and agony over another world, the world of the humans, formerly known as Terra. However the planet is now being used as a place where both clans throw away their scraps, criminals and traitors, as well as it still acts as the no man's land. This has given a new name to this once beautiful world, a name that would scare every citizen of the clans into obedience. This world is now called Exile.

This is the origin story of The Crimson Reaper, Raze. Before all the hatred, before all the killing, before the use of his powerful scythe, and back when he had another name. Back then he was a normal human boy, who lived happily in a small town that was almost completely cut off from the rest of the world. His name was Nihilanth 'N' Spirit.

# *<u>Prologue I</u>*

# *<u>1</u>*

The war has been going on for over a century now, the world has now seen the true colors of both sides now. Or at least they have had the time for it.

I have been around for millenia, yet I have not once in my entire life reached my desired goal, it is the same goal as every ruler in any world, world conquest. I am the perfect manifestation of a conqueror. If that was not the case then I would not have the power that I posses right now.

For unlike some people in this world, my world and the other one, I was never born a powerful person. I was born a weakling, a good for nothing bastard and an outcast. Everything I have now I had to earn. I had to fight, steal and kill without mercy or compassion for others.

But now I am here, and I will do my predecessor one better by doing the one thing that he could not during his time. I am going to patrol my armies around this entire world, and every other. With that I am going to be the one and only supreme leader of all existence. But in order to reach that goal, I have to win the war by destroying my enemy. That is why I am here.

"Sire!" I heard a voice shout through the trees behind me, as it slowly approached and got closer.

"Yes, what is it." I responded without turning around to face the man.

"Forgive me for disturbing you. But it's finished." He said, this time he was standing still.

"Is it really finished already? Very well, you're forgiven for the disturbance. Now, I shall go and see it for myself. Would you mind accompanying me?" I said, as I turned around and slowly walked towards the trees that the man had come from. The man was no ordinary one, he had a lion's tail sticking out of his back, and lion ears sticking out of the top of his head. He was yet to have a lion's mane, that would not show properly until he had finished his trial. As I walked towards him, he responded with.

"I would be honored to do so, my Emperor." He said.

After a short walk through the large trees, we arrived at our destination. A large lake with growing grass, tall trees, boulders and piles of rocks around it. Not far from the lake was the bottom of the cliff that I had been staring from recently.

This is where my tool for success would manifest, if done properly of course.

I walked over to the water and dipped my hands into it. There was a burning sensation of pure chaos and rage. It is exactly what I was hoping for.

"You have done a fine work my friend. Of course I expected no less from you." I said, while smiling and looking at the lion man.

"It was my pleasure sire. I'm honored to serve you." He said while bowing forward.

"You're as loyal as ever. I'll be sure to reward you handsomely." I said, with another smile.

"I'm very grateful to you sire... I hope that you don't mind me asking, but... What is all of this for exactly?" He said while having his arm over his chest. If you looked closely you would notice his tail wagging and his ears twitching.

"Oh this is all for world conquest, my friend." I said with a melody.

"Yes, I know that. But how exactly?" He asked.

"Well, let me ask you this. Who is it that truly participate and win wars?" I said.

"Well sire, the soldiers do." He answered, and he was correct.

"Indeed. So if soldiers win wars, then we need ours to be stronger than every other. We also need an expendable amount of them. What we have done here is making sure that there will be more demons like us." I said. The lion man's eyes opened wide.

"I see, this lake slowly but certainly turns everything it comes in contact with into a demon. It even has a greater effect on humans." He said. He now understands what my plan was.

"Yes. The humans will be turned into demons, and thus The Divine will run in and try to kill them.

Those who survive will join us, in an effort to destroy The Divine." I said with a proud voice. I was sure that my plan was flawless, but the lion man then said something that almost made me worry.

"What a magnificent plan sire! But there's one thing that you will get along the way with this plan." He said.

"Oh really. What might that be?" I asked.

"It will increase the chance of you finding your Unum." He answered. His answer shocked me for a bit. I was relieved that it was just this that he was referring to, but I did not think that he would know about that effort.

Unum was the title given to the demon who is to take the throne of Demon Emperor, when the current one decides to leave the throne and rest eternally.

The Demon Emperor's throne is not passed down among the family. The Emperor can still have a family as he wishes, but his children will never be born to sit on the throne. In order to become a Unum one had to first awaken their power, upon that they would become candidates for the title of demon lord. Next they had to earn a spot of a Demon Lord, and the only way to do that was to impress the emperor by either completing a quest that he gives you or offer him something filled with glory. Once they have become Demon Lords they have to fight each other to the death for the title and honor of Unum. The Unum can always be challenged by other Demon Lords for the title, but that can only be done with the permission of both the emperor and Unum themselves.

I was the last Unum, and I got challenged by many for the title. But I never turned a single one down. I had to fight for this, I was smarter, stronger and more tactical than any other demon lord.

"You're smarter than I thought, I might need to promote you." I said and he bowed in appreciation.

It was true, this way I could find my Unum. But this was nothing new to me, for I had already planned this. Not to make many potential Unum, but to make one guaranteed one. He will be stronger than anyone who has ever lived.

## <u>2</u>

The breeze is cold, yet stimulating. There are trees, boulders, animals running around and flowers in different colors. It is all enjoyable, except that the flowers are all so different from each other.

I cannot believe that this is a warzone. This war has gone on for centuries now. But I have only lived for two decades. I was not the one who witnessed the beginning of this war, that one belongs to my grandfather, one of the greatest Divine Kings in history.

"My lord, it's done." Said a Divine man, who bowed before me after passing through some trees to get to me.

"Very well, let's have a look." I said while walking towards the open field, where not a single tree grew but instead was rich in wild wheat. As I arrived upon the field I could already feel it. The relaxing sensation of pure order and peace.

"It's perfect. Well done my kin. Now we can continue our quest of purification." I said with a proud voice.

"Ah, yes my lord... That reminds me... What exactly is our plan with this?" He asked.

I took a deep breath and tried to explain to him.

"We as the divine are the perfect creatures. Nothing else in the world can match us. But as the perfect creatures we have a duty to make sure that everyone is perfect." I said with a proud voice.

"Yes my lord. I know that, it's the main goal of us divine." He said.

"That's very true.This infected soil will one day house farms. Humans will eat whatever grows on those farms. We are divine, we don't hate humans but they are still impure. However that can change." I said, and then stopped for breath, before continuing.

"When the humans eat whatever they grow, they will become infected. That way they will turn into divine. Or at least a part of them will. When that happens we will come in and force them to have children with either each other, or a divine. Once that is done we will kill all the human parents and raise their children in special camps. After that is done we will repeat the cycle until every single trace of human is gone." I said.

"My lord that is a brilliant plan, and there's one thing that you didn't account for in this." He said. I looked at him with a confident look and, with a melody, said.

"Oh please, my plan is flawless. What could I have missed?" To which he answered.

"My lord, the constant creation of new divine will increase the chance of 'To éna' to be born." He said. His answer shocked me. I had not thought about that.

'To éna' is the name that belongs to the hero of the divine. He is said to be so powerful that he can cleanse all evil and impurity from a world by snapping his fingers. He is more than just a story, To éna has existed once many millennia ago, and during that time he cleansed countless worlds. Thus creating our Divine realm.

Many of our divine citizens have been praying for the next To éna to arrive and end the war between us and the demons, the most impure and unforgiven creatures. He has been gone for so long now, if there is one time that he should arrive it is now.

I want to believe that he will arrive and help us on our eternal quest. However, I originally had my doubts about it. To éna is an important hero for our kingdom, but we do not know anything about him. The only thing that we do know is that he is powerful, and that is it.

We do not know how he is born, or what causes him to be born. We are not even fully sure of what he is. As far as we know there could already be a To éna out there, and we do not know it. On top of everything, we do not know if there can be more than one To éna at once.

However, if this plan gives birth to a new To éna by accident, our problems will be solved completely.

"Yeah, you're right. This method might create a To éna. Lets just hope that it does." I said with a broad smile.

# ***Chapter 1: A normal day in the world of traitors***

## **1**

Running through the huge wheatfields of a beautiful land. Being covered by the sun's rays, farther bringing out the color and glow of the massive golden field. Feeling a slight wind, making everything turn and put a little chill on his skin, was a small boy wearing a gray roughed out tunic, with black hair, black eyes, and a broad smile as he was looking for his friend who was hiding somewhere in this golden field.

"Perdita, where are you? I'm going to catch you!" He said with a soft and joyful voice. The black haired boy looked around, keeping his eyes and ears peeled, until he heard a loud rustle behind him and put on an even broader smile.

"You know I will!" He said as he, with full speed and all the power in his legs, ran and then leaped on to the source of the loud noise and screamed.

"Haha... I caught y- ....". He stopped himself realizing that he had only caught a small chicken.

"Hehehe... Oh you are so silly, you fell for it again" A small girl with brown hair, brown eyes, wearing a pink dress and being about the same age as the boy, stepped out of hiding behind a giant rolled up stack of wheat.

"Dammit Perdita, It's no fun with your tricks" The boy said with a disappointed look.

"Well It was shame on me for fooling you once, but you got fooled by the exact same trick twice so this time it's very much shame on you Spirit" The girl said with a wide smile.

"....."

Spirit did not respond to that, for a short while there was an awkward silence filling the open space of stepped on wheat that they were standing in.

"Well I guess you're right about that, it kind of was my own fault for falling for it again." Spirit said breaking the complete silence between them.

"But next time I won't fall for your tricks." He then added, with a completely serious look on his face. Perdita just laughed silently and said:

"Alright whatever, I would love to see you try."

"Anyway we should get back to the village, my father is probably looking for me" She said, looking off into the distance.

"Yeah you're right, mine is probably doing the same by now." Spirit responded while standing up and looking off in the same direction. In the distance of that direction was their town, Siligo, and the three huge walls that separates the areas of the different classes.

. . .

Siligo was a town with giant wheat farms surrounding it. The wheat is special for it gives the flour and bread a taint of gold.

The town's market district was as lively as ever, flour and bread shops along the street. Children like our young, ten year old, Spirit and Perdita were running around, some of them with either red apples or golden tinged bread in their hands or in small baskets, and farmers with their scythes going out or coming home from the fields.

Spirit took a long look at the farmers, with a visible expression of disappointment.

"What's that look for? Did you expect something special from the them?" said Perdita with an expression of curiosity.

"No, that's not it at all." Answered Spirit, with his hands waving in the air.

"It's just that one day that will be me going off to the field, and I just don't want that. No, I don't want to spend my entire life sowing wheat all day, I want something bigger for my life." He then said looking up in to the sky.

"Well, you are not the only who thinks that way." Said Perdita, while looking down into the ground.

"My life has basically already been laid out for me to follow, and I don't want that in the least. I want go out and see how the world is outside of this village, but I can't do that, my father won't let me do anything that I want" She then said looking off into the same direction. She then turned her head towards Spirit and said:

"I'm surprised that you are complaining about your life, Spirit. Your father basically lets you do whatever you want to do. You could have gone for a swim in the woods earlier and your father would be okay with It."

"Oh, so you like swimming now all of a sudden." He answered with a grin.

"My father does give me a lot of freedom, but he still has me working on the farm a few days straight at best. He's only training me to become a farmer for the rest of my life, because he's making me work more and more as time passes. Haven't you noticed that we don't get to see and play with each other as much recently?" Spirit then said looking at Pedita with a serious face.

"Yeah, you're right. I'm sorry, I forgot about the fact that you have to work like hell to feed yourself." Perdita said looking down at the ground.

"It's alright, my life isn't as terrible as I make It sound. I just want to be in control of my destiny for once." He then said, quite emotionally, while looking at Perdita.

"Yeah, I feel the same as you. I want to decide and be the kind of person that only I want to be." Perdita said, looking at Spirit with the exact same expression as him.

"Well, I'm glad that we understand each other and want the same thing for our lives. However, how we go about to get what we want in our lives will be completely different for the two of us. We might have to split off from one another, or make a hard life decision in order to get what we desire. I'm sure that you understand that as much as I do, Perdita." Spirit then said with the same serious face as before.

"I do, however. If you ever get in trouble, I promise I will help you out." She then said with a worried face.

"Alright, then I promise to help you too." He said with a proud face.

"You really mean it?" Perdita asked with a sad and worried look.

"Of course I do, I promise that I'll be there for you if you ever need It." Spirit said smiling and placing his right hand on Perdita's head.

"Thank you" Perdita said quietly looking into Spirit's eyes.

"Now then, we should get back to our parents for now, don't you think?" He said with a smile.

"Yeah, we got carried away didn't we." She said, also smiling.

"We really did, so we should probably hurry home." Spirit said as they took off to their homes with new dreams, and important promises made.

They walked straight past all the stands, and most of the houses, until they got to the gate of the huge three-part wall, where they had to split off from each other and walk in two different directions.

"Well, I guess I'll see you some other time then." Perdita said.

"Yeah, we'll have to see when that will be." Spirit answered as they split off from each other and walked through different gates to get to their homes, which were placed on two different sides of the town.

For Spirit the road back was not that long from where they split off, however the lack of company made it feel like it took ages until he would get back.

He just had so many thoughts in his head while walking:

*Will I ever get my freedom? What can I do instead? Do I have to lose Perdita in order to gain It? Will I be able to keep my promise to her?*

He thought while still walking home, but then stopped thinking about that because he realized that his father might put him to work when he gets back.

Upon arriving at his own doorstep, the door immediately was flung open by a large and muscular male with black hair and a beard. He looked straight at Spirit with a smile and said:

"Ah, so you're home already my son."

"Yes father, I am home now. Are we going to the field?" Spirit said with a pretended smile while he actually was feeling disappointed.

"No, we are not going to the field today." His father answered, still smiling.

"Huh? Then where are we going?" Spirit asked while being completely confused for a while.

"Today we are going to go fishing for dinner. I have already done what was needed to be done on the field today." He said looking down at his son.

"That sounds fun and interesting." Spirit said now smiling.

"It does indeed. Now, shall we get going then, my son?" His father said while still smiling and looking at Spirit.

"Yes! Let's go!" Spirit said with a smile as he followed his father through the woods and to a lake, with a fishing rod on his shoulder.

Spirit was very surprised by this, his father suddenly wanted to go fishing with him instead of working. Were they just going to spend some time together, or did his father have something special in mind for him.

*Whatever! We are gonna go out and catch some fish. It's going to be fun, and even if he does have something special in mind then I'll take it head on.*

Spirit thought as he was still walking alongside his father, both with broad smiles on their faces. Not having a care in the world about what is happening around them, and outside the village.

# <u>2</u>

*He is always so happy, he has everything he could want, he has freedom.*

That's how she used to think at least. Now she has realized that he lives behind his own prison bars, not being able to control his fate in any way. That fact was reinforced by his family's poverty, and yet he still promised to help her in danger.

Those thoughts ran through Perdita's head as she was walking all the way home. No matter how much she tried, she simply could not think about anything else. He was filling every deep corner of her mind and there was nothing she could do to stop it. Just the thought of Spirit making such a big promise to her while he barely could keep his family fed. He was so poor, yet still promised her that.

However, another thought raced through Perdita's mind, it was about her father. If he found out that she was playing with a poor boy from a farmer family he would get really mad and would punish her, right after lighting Spirit's house on fire. The worry wouldn't stop flowing through her.

*Spirit has enough trouble as it is. If father finds out about him, it would be even worse than the worst.*

She thought while still walking past the houses in the noble area. Every house was over two-stories high and were either made of fine stone or marble. After a while she stopped outside of a white marble house and walked towards it.

Upon arriving at its doorstep, Perdita felt a little nervous about going through the door. However, she bit her teeth together and walked through only to be greeted by her father.

"Now, where have you been Perdita?" Said her father, showing no expression what so ever.

"I was just out and wandering." Perdita answered, with a trembling voice.

"All alone?" Asked her father.

"Y- yes" Answered Perdita, her voice trembling even more this time.

"Hmm ... alright then, let me know when you go out next time. Now go up to your room and change your outfit, it's time for teaching and your mother is waiting for you in the dining room." Her father said, with an expression of suspicion.

After their conversation, Perdita walked up to her room. While browsing through the different colored dresses in her closet she started daydreaming about her future, about her freedom and her life in a small house next to the wide ocean.

She thought about it long and hard, and then she suddenly got a strange feeling as she saw a male figure dressed in a black and crimson red coat holding out his hand to her. Even though she could not see the man's face for it was clouded over by a shadow, she stretched out to grab the man's hand.

"Perdita! ...Hurry up already!" A loud voice yelled, knocking Perdita out of her dreams and into reality again.

"Yes mother, I'll be right there." She answered with a shock from her mother's shout.

After that Perdita just picked the first dress that she saw and hurried changing before running downstairs to greet her mother.

# 3

*Well, this was an unexpected surprise.*

I thought as I followed behind a strong, wise and very kind man. The same man that I've been looking up to my entire life, the man who helped me through every hardship in my life and kept teaching me about how to be a farmer, so that I one day could take his place in that.

This man was Nihilanth 'N' Warden, a man said to be a former warrior who risked his life for people in need, and was said to be the world's strongest warrior with every possible weapon, tool and martial art. However I did not recognise him for any of that. For I knew him as nothing more than father.

Today was just weird, we never get to do this and just walk out into the woods, leaving all the work undone. However, he did say that all the necessary work was already finished. This probably means that he'll only want to lecture me about important things in nature, and not just enjoy a trip of fishing without any disturbance...

"Alright we're here!" Father said, knocking me of my train of thought. We were at a giant lake with long strands of grass sticking out of almost all edges. Except for the one spot that we were at, a pile of huge rocks that showed no sign of moving no matter what you tried. Around the lake there were tall trees and many piles of rocks in different areas.

"This lake is known for it's good catches. The fish tend to grow so large that the fishermen sometimes bring horse carriages that fit almost six large men, and they still only manage to hold one fish at a time." He then said looking at me. My mind almost went blank. Fish that is bigger than six fully grown men. What kind of monsters live in this lake?

"But... How do they even manage to catch those beasts? And how did they even grow so damn large in the first place?" I said with with eyes and ears wide open, unable to comprehend what they have been told. Then father, with a smile on his face, calmly responded by saying:

"They're not normal fishermen catching those behemoths. They're specially trained to be strong enough to do it. Instead of fishing rods and lines, they use spears and giant hooks to do it. Even with training and equipment it still requires at least four men to make the catch. As for why the fish grow so large, nobody is really sure. Most people believe that it's because of some substance from The Demon empire."

"Oh right, The Demon empire. You told me about them." The demon empire is the homeworld of the demons. It's said that they are ruthless warriors with unimaginable strength and power. It's also said that they often are huge monsters that many people often refer as 'Mutated messes'. So if it was some sort of demonic substance that, for some odd reason, had leaked into this lake I really wouldn't be surprised at all. However that is very unlikely.

"Yes I did, I'm glad that you remember...Anyway, while it would make sense for it to be some demonic substance, I really doubt it. This lake has been like this for almost twenty years now, and if it really has been some demonic substance all this time then why haven't The Divine kingdom investigated it yet." He said now looking down at the lake without showing me his face.

"The divine kingdom. You have told me about them as well."

The Divine kingdom are said to be the greatest enemies of The Demon empire. It's also said that they are elegant people who live elegant lives. They have soldiers that, instead of relying on their pure strength, rely on their difficult and complex martial arts that is based of their unique ability.

Nobody truly knows what this ability is, how it works or where it comes from, but right now there are people thinking that the unknown divine, or angel, ability is based of light elements. Because of this theory the divine have earned the nickname 'Light bulbs'. Which I think is more humiliating than being called 'Mutated mess'.

"You really believe that The demons and divine exist?" I asked with a cold look. The demons and divine where nothing but a fairy tale that adults tell their kids in order to make them behave.

"Well yes, according to the tales they have been at war for ages and they have caused a lot of pain upon others." He said with a curious look.

"How can you believe in such things? Have you ever seen a demon or a divine for yourself?" I asked, with a loud voice.

"Well no, it's just that it's too good to not be true." He said.

"Father, you're saying that you believe that magic is what created the behemoths in this lake rather than an explanation based on fact and reason." I said, keeping my cold glare at father.

Father then put his hand behind his head, and laughed it off by saying.

"Yeah, you're right. It's just a fairy tale and nothing more."

I exhaled and, in return, put my hand behind my head and said.

"Yeah, sorry for yelling." After I said that we both laughed, and I asked father something that I had been confused about since the start of our fishing trip.

"But wait, if the fish in this lake are so big and difficult to catch. Why are we here at this lake to fish? I mean you're strong, really strong. But I don't think that we'll be able to catch a behemoth like that."

Father then looked at me with a weird face and said.

"Hahaha... You sound so silly now." He said with tears in his eyes from the laughing. His response annoyed me a lot, so my voice was automatically full of anger as I responded with:

"Why? What's so funny!"

Father then looked at me, still smiling and said:

"Tell me, does this forest only have bears running around ? No. If that was the case then there would be nothing to hunt in these forests. Hell, if there were bears and nothing else they probably wouldn't stay for too long since they would have nothing to feed on." He said waving his hands around while still holding the fishing rod. Then he continued with:

"The fish grow abnormally large here, yes. But they pray on smaller fish in order to do so. However, those fishes are also quite big and strong so therefore I have gotten ahold of these special fishing rods. They are made out of iron while still being flexible, and at the end hangs a small metal rope instead of a thin string."

"Alright then, you could have just said that." I said, still annoyed, with a changed tone in my voice.

"Come on! Cheer up son, lets catch some fish now." He said as he was handing me a rod. At that moment I simply couldn't help but smile and grab on the the rod and say:

"Alright then, let's catch a behemoth or two."
To which he responded with:

"Yeah, that's how it's done Spirit!"

# <u>4</u>

One hour, at least, had passed and still nothing biting on the line. I was almost considering giving up until father asked me:

"Hey son, be honest with me now. What do you wanna do with your life when you grow up? Because it clearly isn't farming."
For a moment I thought that my heart was going to explode out of stress.

*How could he have known about that?* I thought to myself for a moment, then took a breath and answered by saying:

"Well, you are right about that one. But it's not that I hate farming, it's just that I want to see the world. I want to travel around and train in different martial arts, meet new people and see new places until I decide to settle down in one spot. I was thinking about doing it with my brothers at first but, you know. One left without notice, and the other tried to kill me over some accident that I didn't have anything to do with at all."

He then looked at me with a half concerned look and said:

"Your brothers? You mean your cousins right? I know how you feel about them, you're angry with both of them. Don't get me wrong, I would be too, but I think it's time to let go of them."

"Oh, I already have. I'm still a bit mad at red-eyes for trying to kill me, but other than that I've completely let go without forgetting." I said while looking right back at father.

"Alright then, that's good to hear. Anyway, about your plans of traveling the world. I want to help you and I think I know the perfect way to do so." He said smiling again.

"Really!? How!?" I responded with excitement.

He then grabbed on tightly to the fishing rod, took a deep breath and said:

"If you are to make it through your journey without getting hurt, you will need to prepare yourself both physically and mentally. In other words you need to train your body and mind. I will help you with that. In less than 10 months I will train you to be perfectly fit for your journey, however it will feel like hell. I gotta be honest, it will be really hard and you might not be able to make it through everything. You think that you're up for it?"

For a moment I had think really hard. If I don't make it through then I might not be able to go at all, but on the other hand if I do make it I might be as strong or maybe stronger than father. I tightened my grip, took a deep breath and said:

"I'll do it!"

"Alright then, if that's the case we'll start right now, by catching some fish. In order practise the mind you must be patient and wait for the fish to bite, and since we're at the lake with behemoths, you'll have to practise your strength in order to reel in the catch." He said this time with a serious face. That's something you don't see every day.

"Oh and by the way. Were you planning to travel around with that friend of yours instead? Perdita was her name right?" He said and almost gave me another heart attack.

"Well, maybe. Why are you asking?" I said, with my voice still trembling from the shock.

"Because if you plan to do so then it will be your job to protect her from everything. But in order to do that you'll need to be strong enough, and in order for that to happen you first need to survive the so called 'purgatory'." He said, looking right at me with that serious look. Now I know that he isn't joking about all this.

He is going to train me, and in order to properly do that he is going to throw me into 'Purgatory of both mind and body'.

# *Interlude I*

# *1*

Classes are so boring. There is nothing fun about anything, and everything is always the same. History, where every tale or conflict ends with the nobles getting the better end of things. Language is the most boring thing ever, all you do is sit still in your chair and repeat different phrases all the damn time.

And, as a bitter cherry on top of the already ruined cake, we never do anything outdoors. We never do any kind of exercise or any kind of outdoor explanation.

"Perdita!! Pay attention!" Ms. Blue yelled at my face, knocking me out of my bitter line of thought about class.

"Yes mam." I responded respectfully, with eyes wide open.

"Good grief, are you tired or are you ignoring me on purpose?" She asked with a calm tone.

Ms. Blue was an old and smart woman. She has apparently been the teacher to many of the successful nobles. This naturally made her very famous, however only the richest could afford an education from her.

According to an unwritten tradition, every noble has to get the best education possible. Although I am surprised that we can even afford this, considering that father's business has been going really bad. I think I heard him say that the cart transporting his goods was sacked by some bandits. I do not know what father will do to fix all this, but I am sure that whatever he does he will not become less strict than he already is.

"No ma'am, I just got lost in thought." I answered calmly, as I sat in my chair with a cup of tea on the small table in front of me.

"Good grief... Alright, we can take a ten minute break if you like." She said with a kind voice.

"Thank you. It would be appreciated." I said as I sunk down into my chair.

When I looked to my right, and through the window, I could see the farmers out harvesting the fields. They are really poor so they do not get to have the luxury of a great education, they do not need that much of an education to do what they do. A part of me pities them for having to bust their asses in order to make their living, but another part of me envies them. They cannot do much with their lives, but at least they do not have to attend to these torturous classes.

My look stopped at on specific point. At a boy who was swinging his scythe and cutting down the wheat. He had black hair and a semi dark skin tone. It was Spirit. Even I can recognize him from this distance, which was a good 400 meters. He was always working his ass off, and still he could manage having a smile on his face.

At that moment I decided that I too would work hard. I will get through these classes, become a respectable noble one day and help Spirit out of his poor life. It would not be nearly as hard as how he works, but I will do whatever I can.

I took another look at Spirit from outside the window, and then looked over at my teacher and said.

"Ms. Blue, we may continue now."

# <u>2</u>

The fields. They bring nothing but the thought of work to mind. The golden wheat of Siligo is the biggest business that we have available. Here I am, whacking away at it so that it later can be turned into flour and be sold. That is how us workers make money.

I looked to my left and saw another boy working alongside me, he was five years older than me and had orange hair. He raised his head and made eye contact with me, before he said.

"Hey Spirit. How you doing?"

"I'm alive. What about you. How are you doing, Joe?" I said holding my scythe straight up with the bottom part resting on the ground.

"I'm fine, I just wished that there wouldn't be so much work." He said while brushing the sweat from his forehead.

"Well, we still have to work so that we can play our part for the community." I said before I took a sip from my water pouch and then passed it over to Joe as he said.

"That's true, but don't you ever wonder what it's like to be a noble?" He asked and then took a sip from the pouch.

"Hell no! I don't care what the nobles do for a living because it's not important." I said with an angry glare.

Joe showed shock in his face as he passed back my water pouch. As I caught it I stared off into the distance and saw a house. It was made out of white marble, with silver and gold decorations. It belonged to a noble, but not just any noble. The one that I happened to be great friends with.

"Hey, Is something wrong." Joe asked with confusion.

"Oh, no. I was just staring at the noble house." I said with a clear voice.

"Okay then. By the way, you and your father contribute a lot to the community." Joe said, quickly changing the subject.

"Well, that's only because father and I do a lot of things." I said, scratching the back of my head.

Just like some nobles own companies with workers, we have communities with our fellow workers.

We all have different jobs, some of us are woodcutters, some are hunters, miners or farmers like me (most of the time). What we do is that we share our goods with each other, and thus making business much better. Most of the time the ones who collect or make the goods do not have to go and sell them themselves, others from the community does it.

Although, we do not get a lot of ground to work with, for almost all of it belongs to the nobles. Most of the farming ground, most of the good mines, the great forests and even some hunting and fishing grounds.

It was true that father and I did a lot of things that contributed to the small community that we had with the others in the working class. That is probably the biggest reason to why my father was chosen to be the leader of our community. Along the way of us doing different things like hunting, fishing, farming and woodcutting, father takes the opportunity to teach me whatever he can.

I looked at the noble house again and noticed someone with brown hair through the window. It was Perdita.

I neither envy or pity her. I do not want her life, where I would have to sit in a chair all day long. I do not pity her either, because I know that she would not last a minute out here.

I cleared my mind and thought that I should get back to work. I grabbed my scythe properly and then gave a nod to Joe who simply responded with.

"Aye." As he also took a stance.

We both pulled our scythes back as we took a deep breath. Then, with all our might, we swung our scythes at the wheat while letting out a long cry.

*Hhhyyyaaaahhhhh!!!!*

# *<u>Chapter 2: Purgatory of both mind and body</u>*

## *<u>1</u>*

My body is on fire, my skin is starting to turn dark and gray, I am crying blood and vomiting almost every hour. On top of that my mind is almost completely shattered to fragments of glass from the lack of sleep, or rest in general. It has been almost a month since my purgatory started, and I am already considering giving up just to get some decent amount of sleep. But I have to push these feelings away and keep going, if I wanna reach my goal then I must fight through every painful moment of this intense and blood soaked training. Today will be another one of those days, because father figured out how to properly train me and finish the necessary daily work at the same time. It involves me dragging and pushing carts instead of having horses do the work, and me plowing the wheat field almost entirely on my own.

However, today is at least a little bit different. Today father asked me to go to the market in the medium district and buy certain items, like spoons, firewood, scythes and sickles for the upcoming harvest, and some other items that could be considered irrelevant.

The training part about this day is that I will have to carry all of this alone the entire way home, and it takes about thirty minutes to walk from my home in the lower district to the market in the medium district without carrying anything on your back. Taking into account that I am already completely exhausted beyond my limit means that this will not be a very good day for me at all.

But I am not one to complain, at the very least I am being spared from having to lift really big and heavy boulders in an effort to build muscle and body mass.

On my way to the gate that separates the different districts, I noticed that all the workers from the lower district, my district, were all staring at me with weird looks. But before I got the chance to determine what type of expressions they had, one of them walked up to me and asked:

"Hey kid! what happened to you? You look like you've been to hell and back."

A question I have been getting alot this past month. I don't blame them though, I really do look like I have been through something horrible. So everytime that question comes up I just politely answer with:

"What do you mean? Don't we all look like that? I'm of the low working class, just like you and the majority of this town. It's not so uncommon for us to look hideous compared to the upper class nobles. We're out in the field, busting our asses all day long, while they get to sit in their comfortable chairs and sip tea all day."

At first it looked like the man was getting a weird look again, but it almost immediately went away and instead he had a smile and said:

"Yeah, you're totally right. Take care little fella." As he walked away with his companions following him behind.

That encounter only lasted for about four minutes. I stood still for a moment and looked up to the blue and clear sky, with a few really small clouds here and there. I was thinking about how I might not be same person when my purgatory is finally over.

I already look different from a month ago so I can almost guarantee that I will look like someone else when I grow older. But my mind is probably the thing that will change the most if anything. I am already showing signs of change, one of them being constant aggression and frustration. How will I think when I get older, can I even get an idea of that?

This purgatory was designed to enforce my mind and body, but in order to do that I will have to break both of them so that they later can be rebuilt with time as something completely different. I have realized that this past month, and it does not sound pleasing in the least. However, I have already decided what I am going to do and there is no turning back now.

With that last thought I took a deep breath and then I walked along towards the market in the medium district.

*This purgatory isn't eternal, but it won't end unless I finish this task already.* Is the last thing that I thought as I, like a marching soldier, with a fast pace kept going without any disturbance at all.

## <u>2</u>

The market was as always full of people from all classes, from the lowest to the almost highest. There were so many people that it was starting to get crowded even on the 2 kilometer long and 15 meter wide street with all of the stands and shops standing up. I was almost finished with my task to collect some items for my family when I saw a very familiar face in the crowd. A face that I had not seen in almost a month, she was wearing a blue dress with white sleeves. It was Perdita, and I think that we noticed each other at the exact same time because the second that I saw her she started waving and said:

"Hey Spirit"

To which I waved back and responded with:

"Hey Perdita, it's been a long time. Hasn't it?"

She got closer to me and then said:

"Yeah, it's been more than a month since we last saw each other right? What have you been up to during all this time."

For a second I was stuck on my words, if I said that father was training me by throwing me through purgatory she would probably freak out. But I didn't get to say anything because she than added:

"Hey Spirit? Are you alright? You look... I mean your skin looks darker or maybe grayer than before. Has something happened to you?"

The classical question came up once again. Well at least I know how to answer to this one.

"Oh, no it's nothing. I have just earned the trademark lower class worker look from all of the field work and plowing that I've been doing this past month." Technically I was not lying by saying that, since a lot of my purgatory training has involved me plowing the fields.

"O- okay, if you say so. I was just wondering, because I know what the workers look like, and you, no offense but you look far worse than some of these workers, and you've gotten that look in such a short amount of time. It's just strange if you ask me." She said as she crossed her arms and shaped a big grin on her face.

"Well, I've had to work really hard. I'm probably at the very lowest of the lowest when it comes to classes." I said with an innocent grin that clearly wasn't convincing enough because of my horrible looks.

"Yeah, I know about your place in the classes, and I'm really sorry for that." She then said looking down at the ground.

"Don't be, I can't say that I'm happy with how things are but at least I'm still alive so I can't complain." I responded with a half serious grin on my completely messed up face.

There was a silence between us for a while and I started to stare off to the small houses and stands around in the area. The houses had stone walls with roofs made out of either brick or grass. These houses were very common in this district and, compared to the ones in my home district, they look very luxurious.

But there are better houses in this town, in the upper class district, or the noble district. I have never been there myself, however, Perdita is one of the nobles and she once told me that all of the houses in that district are at least two stories tall, with brick roofs and walls made out of fine brick stone or marble. It is really hard to imagine, but I know that their houses are much better than all the others, and I have seen some of them so I can't really say much about it.

Our silence was then broken by Perdita when she asked:

"Anyway, what are you doing here?"

I was sort of surprised but ignored it and answered with:

"I'm here shopping things that will be necessary for the future with my work. What about you? What is a medium-ranked noble girl doing in a huge dump like this?" To be completely honest it was really weird. The nobles rarely leave their secluded and luxurious district, they even have their own market according to Perdita. So why is she here at all?

"Well, the thing is that I get really tired of being in my own district. I know it sounds weird, but I really don't like being there. Everyone is so spoiled and power hungry, it makes me sick sometimes." She said, looking of to the right with a completely neutral expression.

"But I also really like coming here, when I do I often get to see you and it makes me really happy because you're my only real friend." She then added with a expression that showed that she was really embarrassed saying that. However, in a way I knew where she was coming from.

Sometimes I too don't like being in my own district, and honestly Perdita was my only friend. Ever since the incident with red-eyes, my brother, I have had a hard time trusting anyone. But then I met Perdita, and it felt like I once again was happy that I had someone that could understand me.

"So, do you want some company during the shopping?" She said breaking my long line of thought.

"Yeah, why not? Just let me carry everything, okay?" I then said lightly.

"Okay. Where are we heading?" She said with a bright tone of excitement in her voice.

"Oh, we need to head to the blacksmith. I need to buy some tools for work." I said returning the excitement with a smile.

It is weird, I was supposed to do this alone but I ended up meeting Perdita and she then joined me on this task. I cannot tell her about my purgatory, if I do I will end up having to deal with her worries, and besides. If her father were to find out about it then it would only mean bad news for both me and my family.

*Please don't tell her. I don't want to have to deal with her worry, her father's wrath, and my purgatory at the same time.*

# <u>3</u>

"Spirit for the love of god, let me help you carry some of those things!" I said because I was really annoyed at him, first he doesn't tell me what has made him look so damn hurt and now he spoils me. It is starting to get annoying. But before I could say it he opened his mouth and said:

"No, I won't let you. For one: if people saw you, a noble girl, carry all of this it would cause a scene and I'd rather not deal with that. Two: I don't trust that you, and your weak noble muscles and bones, are strong enough to be able to carry any of this for even a minute. Sorry, but I'd rather carry all of this without help than carry all of this AND you."
He said that with a grin, he was really serious about all of this. However, he still managed to piss me off even more than I already was(I did not think it was possible).

"Christ, you're almost spoiling me more than everyone in the noble district."

"Well, I'd rather annoy you than carry you. By the way, we'll have to part ways at the gate between the districts." He then said changing the subject way to fast.

"What? Why?" I asked with complete confusion in my head.

"You really don't know why? You simply can't come with me to the lower district, for anybody who'd see you would start chasing you like hell. It's like throwing a piece of meat into a pond full of piranhas. I can't follow you into the noble district for the exact same reason." He said with another serious grin on his face. He wasn't just serious this time, he was starting to get angry. I have not seen him angry in a very long time.

"Well, I guess you're right but that only means that we'll part ways for now and meet some other time. Right?" I said with a trembling voice and looking straight into the ground.

"Yeah of course, and I do intend to keep the promise that I made you. Remember." He said with a smile.

*How can he still smile after all the things that he has been through?*

Even with everything in his life being the way it is, his work being a physical and mental hazard, him living in the lowest possible class and he almost has no possessions that he can truly call his. He still manages to smile through all that. I can't imagine the pain he goes through every day just to make a living, we are only 10 years old and he is forced to work endlessly every day while his body gets completely torn to pieces.

My line of thought was broken by our arrival at the gate that seperated all of the districts. The gate was similar to huge walls, with entrances and access to all the different districts. They were big stone walls with runic engravings and torches hanging off the sides of it. I took one good glance at it before I looked back at Spirit and said:

"Well I guess this is it then, I'll see you later."

"Yeah, seeya." He responded with as he walked the opposite way that I was walking

. . .

Later when I arrived at my house I was greeted by my mother who said nothing but:

"Perdita, your father is waiting for you in the living room"

"Yes mother" I said as slowly walked into the living room where father was sitting in his chair, with a cup of tea, next to the fireplace.

"Perdita come here and sit down" He said with no expression on his face that was covered up half way by the shadow.

"Tell me, where were you now?" He asked to which I simply responded with.

"I was out on a walk."

"A walk huh, you were alone I suppose." He said with a grin on his face.

"Y- yes I was, father."

"Well, perhaps you were. But you weren't. You were with that low-class farmer boy, Nihilanth 'N'

Spirit." He said with an empowered voice and a much worse grin than before.

"No, I was alone father. I swear." I said with an even more trembling voice.

"Don't you dare lie to me. You'll stay away from that filthy low-class scum." He said standing up and grabbing me by the arm.

"He's not like th-" I could not finish my sentence over father swinging his powerful hand over my cheek as hard as he possibly could and making a loud snapping sound.

*Pdf!*

After the sound I could feel a burning sensation in that same spot and I let out a loud

"Ahhh!" In a really bright pitch-tone.

"Silence!!! you will not disobey me!" He yelled at the top of his lungs and then continued with

"I will not punish you anymore, your husband will have to do that next week."

"What!" I screamed with tears in my eyes.

"In one week you will marry a boy, the son of a high-class noble." He said now with his back turned against me.

"B-but"

"No buts, you will do this, it is your duty" He said without letting me finish my sentence.

I was completely shocked and with tears in my eyes I ran up the stairs and went straight into my room and cried an entire ocean. I could not think of anything, I was completely ruined. In a week I was going to get married away to someone that I have never even met before, and on top of that father now knows about Spirit and he will surely not let him live peacefully now. It is all my fault, I caused so much trouble for him.

*Spirit I am so sorry, please forgive me.*

# 4

"Come on son you gotta keep going, don't give in just yet." Father yelled as he was trying to motivate me through doing push-ups with a boulder the size of a dinner table on my back. The most painful and annoying thing about this purgatory.

"Y-you-you know that I really hate doing this specifically, don't you?" I said trying to catch for breath as pressed my body upwards for the hundred and fourth time.

"Well, yeah sort of. But I did tell that it was going to be painful and that I was going to train your mind as well, didn't I?" He said, looking down at me with one of the widest smiles that I have ever seen. Only Nihilanth 'N' Warden could possibly pull of such a great smile with so little effort.

"One Hundred-five... One Hundred-six... One Hundred-seven!!" I was slowly counting my way up the most horrible ladder of pain ever. But when I reached one hundred and ten, father ordered me to stop and stand up again.

But before he could explain what the next task was, we were interrupted by a loud noise coming from our house. The noise appeared to be a man yelling 'NIHILANTH!!!' at the very top of his lungs.

Showing a big sign of confusion, both father and I ran out of the forest and back to our house to see what all the commotion was all about.

When we arrived at the house there was a semi-elderly man, dressed in a noble's clothing, standing in front of our house with about six armed men behind him. As he caught the glimpse of us, he started charging our way while yelling:

"Nihilanth! Where is she!"

"Wha-what, excuse me who are you and what in hell are you talking about?" Father said with a tense expression, he himself was starting to lose his temper and patience with the man.

"You know what I'm talking about. Where is my daughter, Perdita?!!!" The man yelled right into my father's face, with each second father's patience was running low as his anger was flying high. But one thing caught my ear when the man yelled.

"Wait, are you Perdita's father? What's wrong? Has something happened to her?" I asked, and the man's face just turned red as he looked at me and said.

"You tell me! She ran away from home last night and the only place that she possibly could have gone to is your misserable little shitshack that you call a house." The man stopped for breath, because yelling is apparently exhausting for him. I looked over at my father and from his expression I could tell that he already had pieced everything together, that Perdita was my friend and that this angry old a-hole was her father.

"Alright, I get where you're coming from but Perdita isn't here because I never showed her my house before so she wouldn't know how to get here in the first place." I said as politely as I could to this man, which is not saying a lot considering how 'polite' he has been.

This whole incident had attracted a lot of people. Before I knew it there was a crowd just wondering what was going on and what a noble man was doing here in the first place.

"Alright then let's say that I do believe you, you wouldn't happen to know where she is? Then you wouldn't mind if we searched your house until we found her?!" The man said with a very angry expression. But unfortunately for him father's patience was growing very short as he walked up to the angry noble man and said.

"You won't be searching my house or any house for that matter. You will just crawl back to the stinking serpent hole that you came from, sit your fat and weak ass down on a chair and drink your bitter cup of tea." Wiser words have never been spoken in this district. But it was not enough to make the man leave, for his face got even more red as he said.

"Oh I will search your house and if I don't find her in there I will search every single house in this district until I find her and when I'm done I will burn all of them to ashes. Nobody will stop me, you know why? Because I'm a noble and you are all a bunch of worthless pese-" He was cut off mid sentence by a hard and loud

*Pdfff!*

Followed by a sound of something cracking. It was caused by my father, he had apparently punched the man's nose so hard that it made that sound and clearly broke something. The man fell to the ground screaming in pain while covering his nose with his hands. After a while he stood up again and yelled to his men

"What are you standing there for?! Get him!" But that only caused some of the other workers watching the fight join the battle to help their fellow man, my father.

"Spirit get out of here now!" Father yelled through all the chaos. I obeyed because I was going to do so anyway, not in order to skip the fight but rather to run around and look for Perdita. Wherever she has run off to, she must be in trouble and she needs my help.

*Perdita don't worry, no matter where you are I will find you and I will not let any harm get to you. Because I intend to keep the promise that I made to you over a month ago.*

# *Interlude II*

*Well this is not going to be pretty.* I thought as I looked straight across from myself and saw the angry grins of six armored men with maces in their hands. Their boss, the old and very angry noble man was standing behind them for cover while still holding his hands over his bleeding nose.

"What are you waiting for, kill him!!!" The old man yelled to his men. I am glad that I sent Spirit away, if he was still here he could have gotten very hurt…

My line of thought was broken by the sight of the armored men raising their maces and getting ready to tackle me.

I raised my own fists but before I could do anything else another seven men raised their fists as well, while they took position next to me on both left and right.

"Hell no! We're not letting you fight this one out by yourself Warden!" One of the men on my right said with a proud voice. After he said that the other men roared in agreement, and I did nothing but say.

"Thank you."

I looked forward again and saw the old man as his face got even redder and yelled.

"Another seven people ain't going to save you from this Warden!" At us.

I looked to my right, and then to my left. Then I, with a proud grin on my face, said.

"Well, I'm not planning to hide old man. I'm not scared of you." The old man took a deep breath through his mouth and then said.

"I'll teach you not to mess with me."

"Is that so? Then come and get me!" I said with a grin on my face as I heard the others roar next to me.

The old man became furious as his face grew even redder than before. He then took his right hand off his face and pointed at me while yelling.

"Get him!!!" To his men, and they obeyed, for as he did they started charging at us full speed with maces in hand. I took a deep breath and yelled.

"Charge!!!" To my fellow workers assisting me in this battle. After a loud battle roar from everyone we charged at the armored men with full force.

I was confident in my abilities so I charged to take on a soldier on my own, while the others would most likely have to find a way to tag team against the others. So I charged at the leading soldier, with all my might and gave him a solid punch to his belly. However it was covered in plate armor so it had almost no effect on the man, for it only tilted him backwards a few centimeters. When he regained his balance he swung his mace towards my face. But it was to no avail for I simply caught the metallic block at the end and ripped out of the man's grip.

Once I had taken a proper grip around the handle of mace I dragged it backwards, and then with my entire body swung it with all of my might at the man's unprotected head. A loud cracking noise could be heard and blood splattered everywhere as the mace hit the man's head so hard that it had completely crushed the upper part of his head. As the sound died out I ripped the mace out of his broken skull, and watched as his corpse toppled over and fell down to the ground.

*That makes one… Only five left*
I thought as I looked around, searching for the next one to attack, as I was breathing heavily. But it does not really look like the others need help. One pair managed to kill one soldier already so they moved on the help take down the remaining four. I did the same and helped another group take out a soldier by smacking him on the neck with my mace and effectively breaking it.

The others made short work out of the remaining three, so I just did the only thing that was left to do before concluding this mess. I walked forward and saw the old man trying to escape, but was stopped by some other workers and thrown to the ground. As I got up to him he clutched his hands together as he, on his knees, prayed to me by saying.

"Please. I'll give you anything, money, power, my whole business, anything."

I just looked down at him with a menacing look, and after taking a deep breath and picking up the old man by the neck, I said.

"I don't want your stupid money or power. I'd love for you to go to hell, but I can't kill you. If I do I will just get more trouble."

The old man looked at me with a desperate look and said.

"Yes exactly. So just let me go and find my daughter and leave this place, and I will never be in your way again."

"I said that I couldn't kill you. That doesn't mean that I can't hurt you. And also I will be taking full protective custody of Perdita, and there's nothing you can do about it." I said with another menacing look and angry voice. The old man looked at me and said.

"But you can't do that, she is my daughter."

"You may be her biological father, but you certainly aren't a parent." I said, with the same powerful voice.

"But-"

"Enough!!! Now I'll show you the might of us workers!!!" I yelled to cut him off. With that he started screaming and begging, but I did not care and threw him down to the ground and started stomping and kicking him. Not long after that the others surrounding us joined me and started stomping at the old man.

After a few minutes of stomping I cleared the crowd and made them all back away. When they all had taken a few steps away, I stepped forward, put my right knee on the old man's chest and, as he was struggling to breathe, I pushed the thumb of my right hand into his right eye socket and with tremendous force ripped his right eye out.

I could hear a loud scream of pain as the old man covered his right eye socket with his bloody hands.

I then stood up and looked at the eye in the palm of my right hand, before I clenched it and destroyed the eye within.

"Take this old fool to the gate guards so that they can carry him back to the noble's district." I said to my men. They obeyed immediately and two men, against their own liking, carried the old man away. I followed them with my eyes as they walked past, and when they were gone I turned to the rest of the workers and said.

"Alright. I think you all know what needs to be done here. We'll have to take these corpses and then burn them in one of the charcoal kilns." The men all responded and got to work immediately.

As I carried one of the corpses with the help of another, I started thinking.

*What happened to Spirit? Is he out and looking for Perdita?*

Were the questions that I asked. But I quickly threw them away. Because, no matter what, I cannot let Spirit or Perdita see these corpses, so we need to get rid of them quickly.

# ***<u>Chapter 3: I told you that I'd keep my promise to you</u>***

# ***<u>1</u>***

*Where in hell could she be?* Is the only thought that I had in my head while running past some rocks and weird trees in the forest. It was huge and vast, so it would almost be impossible to try and find her alone. Still, have to try. Because if I don't then my father, along with the rest of my district, will suffer and get hurt, or worse. But there is something I still do not understand. Why did she run away in the first place? I do understand one part of it at least, if I lived with that annoying old man as my father I would have left a very long time ago. She would have as well. So what happened.

I stopped running for a second so that I could try to figure out why. It did not seem like something had happened to her when we met at the market yesterday. So it must have happened afterwards. But what could it be. Another thing that is really confusing is how her father knew my name, and that he came to my home specifically in order to search for her-

Wait... Could it be that he found out that I was Perdita's friend. Damn that is bad, I knew that by seeing Perdita I would put me and my family in danger. The nobles are not exactly happy that their kids spend time with the worker-class kids. But he is taking it really far, it is like his life will be over if he does not have Perdita. All the nobles have some sort of income that feeds off the worker-class. But what was his again?...

Yeah, that is right he was a owner of a metal trading company with workers working day and night in the mines. But Perdita told me a while ago that his last delivery got robbed and that he lost a lot of money because of that, and was now going bankrupt. But what does that have to do with Perdi-...

*oh god.* Was the only thought that came to my head after my realization.

The nobles and the citizens in the medium district always try to marry their children to either a richer, or an equally rich, family. So the old man must have promised a richer noble family that he would marry away Perdita to them in order to save his own nobility. It adds up even more when you consider that when nobles marry their children away the girl is always very young. Perdita ran away in order to escape that. I have to find her, fast. Then afterwards that old bastard is going to pay for this.

I felt something really hard curling up in my hand. It was my clenched fist, I must have clenched it subconsciously thanks to all the anger and rage inside my mind.

After I calmed myself I lifted my leg in order to start running again, but at that exact moment I noticed something in the ground. It was something embedded into the ground with a weird shape.

"Tracks!" I shouted in accomplishment, and after examining them I set my route ready to run until I noticed something else.

It was another set of tracks, heading in the exact same direction that Perdita was running. It was a track that I was familiar with, that of a bear. But in a way it was different, it was too big. Not only that, it was headed in the same direction as Perdita.

*Crap! I need to hurry up and find her!* I thought as I took off running again. If that bear, or whatever that thing was, gets to Perdita before I do, it will be really bad. She might get injured, or maybe even worse.

*Come on! Run faster dammit! It's nothing compared to the purgatory so move!!!*

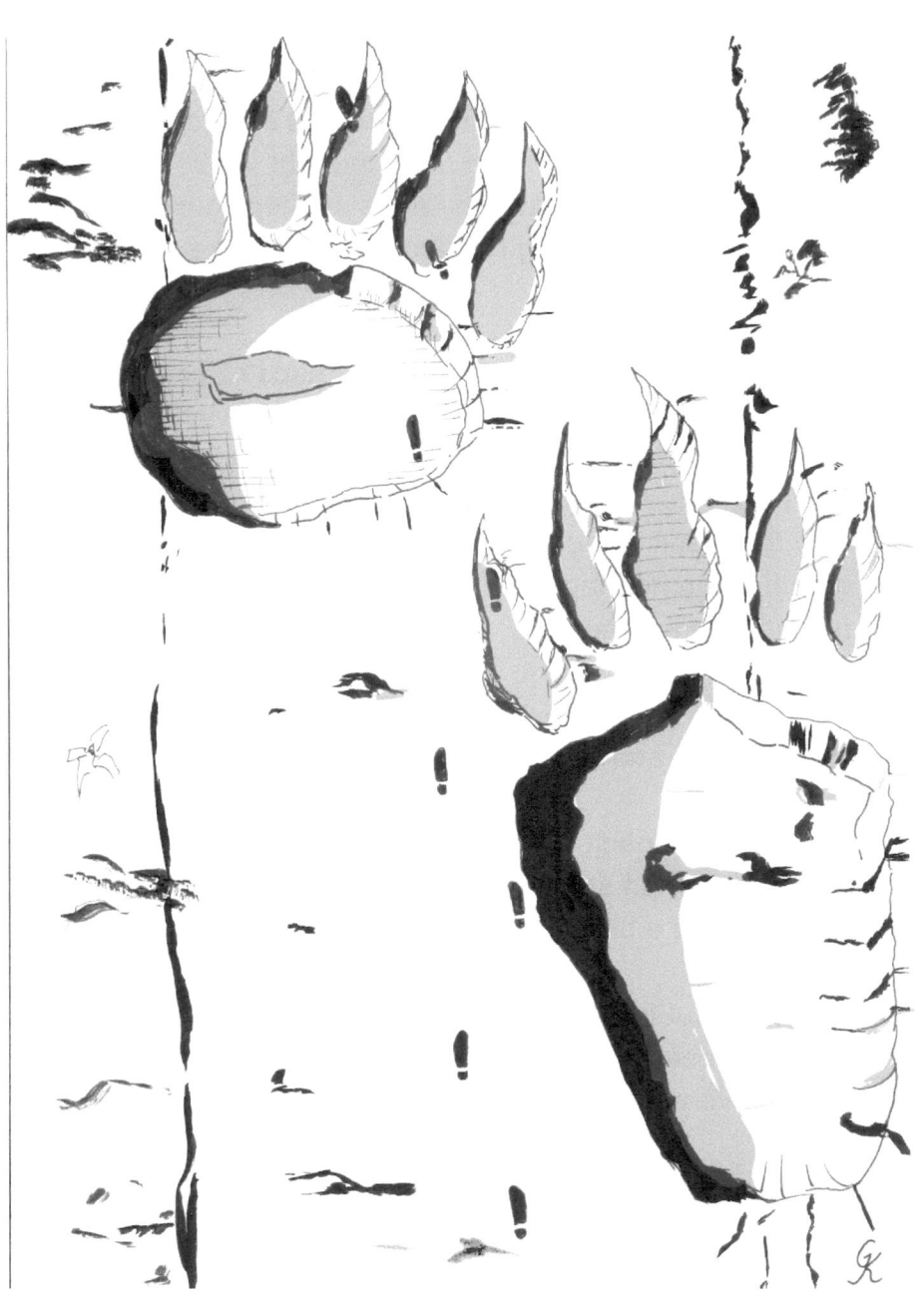

## 2

*It is all my fault. Spirit will suffer and it is all because of me. I'm so sorry. Forgive me.* I thought  as I sat on a branch of a tree with my arms and legs curled up and my head resting on them, as I cried like a baby.

I do not get it. Why am I weeping so much? Spirit is my friend, but why did I run away when knowing that I had caused him trouble. Ever since I first met him I have had a strange feeling about him, and not only that but it has gotten stronger ever since last month when he made me that promise after we played hide and seek.

As I sat in my tree, next to a huge pile of boulders, I kept thinking and weeping. Until I closed my eyes.

I was at that beach cabin again, with the young dark haired man stretching out his hand to me. His face was still a bit blurred.

I reached out for his hand and once I grabbed it and got closer his face became clearer, and I could not believe what I saw. He had dark eyes, a semi dark skin tone with a faint gray, and a smile that I would recognize anywhere.

"S-Spirit?" I said quietly in shock. But then like a bubble popping I woke up from the dream. I was still shocked, was the young man in my dreams really Spirit? If so then does that mean that I-I have been falling for him. I now know why I got so upset when my father found out about him, I now know why I got so upset when I saw him hurt from his work and I now know why I got upset and ran away when father said that I was getting married with someone that I have never met. I am in love with Spirit.

As I made that conclusion I buried myself into my legs once more. Yes, I was in love with Spirit, but right now that is not a happy thing because he probably hates me if he is still alive. Whether I go back or stay away from my family, I will not be able to see him ever again. I will just have to forget about him completely, even if I do not want to, I have to.

For a moment there was complete silence, until I heard a voice call my name.

"Perdita! Perdita it's me" That voice was the one that I tried to forget and as I looked down I could see him.

"Spirit!" I yelled back at him with tears in my eyes. He had found me, gone through all of this trouble just to find me.

"Perdita come down here. Please, we have to go back" He said with a concerned face.

"No, I can't...Why are you helping me? I did nothing but cause you trouble, so are you helping me even though you hate me?" I said with my my voice trembling and on the verge of crying.

"Wha-What makes you think that I hate you? You're my best friend, I could never hate you. So please, come back." He said with a smile on his face. I looked down and could not help but to cry.

After I stopped crying I slowly climbed down the tree, hugged Spirit and cried into his shoulder.

"It's okay." He said with a calm voice.

"I think I know everything now, your father was forcing you into a marriage so you ran away. Correct?" He asked while looking right at me.

"Yes" I responded without looking back at him.

"Don't worry I won't let anything happen to you, okay." He said while hugging me back even harder than I did.

"Thank you" I said with nothing but pure happiness in my voice. I was going to ask if we could stay like this for a moment, but before I could open my mouth he said.

"We have to back now. I'm not sure, but I don't think that we are alo-" He said but he got interrupted by the sound of a loud roar that came from his right. As the source stepped out of the darkness we could clearly see what it was. A monstrously-big animal with black and red fur, claws, huge fangs and spikes running along it's back. At first we both thought that it was a bear, but it was too big and looked way too different. My body had turned to stone, I simply could not move because of pure terror that had struck me. But before I could think of anything else Spirit grabbed on to my arm and dragged me behind him as he started to run away from the bear while yelling.

"WE HAVE TO RUN NOW!!! FOLLOW ME!!!"

# 3

*Goddammit! This is what I was worried about!*

I held Perdita's hand as hard as I possibly could, and then I ran as fast as possible, almost dragging her behind me.

*That thing, whatever that thing was it was not a bear. I know what a bear looks like and for starters they are not that huge. On top of that, they do not have spikes running down their backs.*

While all of these angry thoughts went through my head I kept on running like nothing else mattered. Until we wound up at the wall of a cliffside, blocking our path

"Dammit! It's a dead end!" I yelled while trying to find another way around it. But right as I finished my scream I turned around and noticed that the bear was approaching, slowly.

This is really bad. On one side there is a cliffside blocking our way, and on the other there is a monster. We have been completely pinned down now, with only one option left.

"Perdita, I want you to stay behind me at all times now. Try to hide behind something so that you won't get harmed when I fight this thing." I said as calmly as I could in this situation. I hate to admit it, but it is the truth that our only chance of getting out of this is by fighting. However, I was the only one capable of doing it since I have gone through training.

There are two problems though, one being that there are not many places for Perdita to hide and two being that I am still really exhausted from everything including my training.

"But Spirit, ar-are you really capable of fighting that thing?" She said with a really trembling voice. She was scared and honestly, so was I.

"I don't know. But I have to try, there's no other way. So hide, and if you see an opening you run away from here as fast as you can." I said trying to keep my cool and not get angry or freak out in any way.

"B-Bu-... Okay" She said, voice still trembling and then she ran back trying to hide behind some boulders. Now that I know that she most likely will be safe I can try to fight that thing.

I picked up a stick and took a martial arts combat pose, with both my hands at the stick that was as long as one and a half arm. As I finished my pose the beast had fully arrived towards me and started growling and drooling as it let out a loud:

*Rawrr!*

I took a deep breath in order to stay calm, and then I leaped at the beast with a wound up attack and let out my own battlecry.

*Hyahhh!*

As my leap finished I swung from my right to my left with all of my might and landed a solid blow on the beast's left cheek. It's head waved about a centimeter to my left, and as it stopped again it let out another.

*Rawrr!*

As it swung it's right paw towards me. I desperately tried to block the attack with my stick but to no avail. The stick broke into pieces and the attack continued on until it hit me across the chest. I flew backwards, about five meters, until I hit the ground with a loud noise. I could feel the pain and terror rush through me as I tried to drag myself up to my feet once again. The beast had scarred me pretty bad, I could clearly see where the claws had struck me, leaving nothing but five huge, lineshaped, fleshwounds.

As I got up to my feet again the bear let out another roar, and charged towards me this time.

I tried blocking again, this time with my arms. But once again it was to no avail, because once the beast had finished it's charge it clenched my right arm inside it's huge jaws. I desperately tried to pull my arm out of it's jaws, but that task would not be easy since the monster's teeth had already sunken into my flesh and completely crushed the bones in my arm. I let out a really loud scream of nothing but pure pain as I bashed my left arm onto the beast's head in order to try and do some damage to it. However, this clearly only angered the monster and made it stand on its rear legs and swing me left and right, until it finally let me go and threw straight into the cliffside wall. As I crashed, with my back, into the wall another loud crunch was heard, only this time I clearly had some broken bones instead of bruises.

"Spirit!!" I heard Perdita scream from my right as she tried to move towards me, before I stopped her by saying.

"Don't! Stay ri-right where you are until this is over." As I said that she stayed put and crouched behind the boulder again, with shaking legs. I tried to get back to my feet by supporting myself to the wall and, after two attempts, it worked. Then, as I got up again, I thought.

*It's over. I can't beat this thing. This is where I die. I'm sorry Perdita... P-Perdita. That is right if I die here without killing that monster then she will die as well...*

*No!!! I won't let that happen! Even if I die I won't let this beast get to her!!! I SWEAR!!!*

As that echoed through my mind I could feel something happening inside my body. While my mind was overflowing with rage, my body was overflowing with something else. It was some kind of heat, like a fire, and the more it spread the stronger I felt and, on top of that, a red glow was starting to emit from parts of my body as well as my eyes, turning my vision crimson red. I let out a really loud.

*HYAHHH!*

As the energi overflowed. Once it reached an unbelievable level I charged the beast while winding up a punch from my left arm. The beast let out another loud roar as I charged it with pure rage flowing through my veins. As my charge finished I punched the beast with all of my might, and as I did I let out another

*HYAHHH!*

When I threw my punch right on the beast's right cheek a bright crimson glow appeared, blinding me and everyone else nearby.

With a loud and powerful blast the area where I had fought the bear exploded and blasted me, back first, into the cliffside again. I looked up in accomplishment as I saw a silhouette of the beast, lying on the ground with its head completely severed from its body. It was over, I won.

# <u>4</u>

"Spirit!!!" I once again heard from my right as Perdita ran from her hiding spot towards me. She then went down on her knees in order to level with me. She put her hand on my left cheek and said.

"Are you okay?! Please tell me that you are still alive!"

"I-I'm fine Perdita, don't worry I just need to rest." I said struggling to talk from all of the wounds. Then with tears in her eyes she said.

"Thank god, I don't know what I'd do if you died. Spirit I-I... Sprit I'm in love with you, and I have been ever since we met" What she said shocked me for a while, but then I accepted it. Because after all...

"Yeah, I feel the same way. I love you too Perdita." It was something that took me a while to realize, but it was true. I was in love with her as well.

"Tha-that makes me so happy." She said, her voice trembling more by the second.

"Hey, it's okay. I told you, didn't I?... I told you that I'd keep my promise to you." I said with a calm voice and then catching a breath from all the exhaustion. Perdita looked at me and finally, after holding those tears in for so long, she pushed her face into my shoulder and started crying like a baby. There was no danger anymore, the monster was dead so we could sit here and rest for a long time without getting disturbed.

Whatever power it was that flowed through me during the battle, I am very thankful for it. For without it, both me and Perdita would be dead now. I would not mind if only I died, but if I ever lost Perdita to anything I would be completely lost and unable to continue. Thank you Perdita. Thank you for shining up my dark and miserable life.

# ***Chapter 4: The Hellfire has been ignited***

## ***1***

*Oh lord, please have mercy on my soul.* Was the only thing that I could think on the way back through the forest.

I have never been religious in my entire life. It was probably because of my father, he has no belief, even though he believes that there is an after life. But I still could not help it.

I could barely walk. My right knee, along with my ribs and almost all bones that were not smashed at this point, was on the absolute brink of breaking into pieces. So I had to lean onto Perdita the entire way, while we walked extremely slowly.

When I looked over at Perdita I could not tell how she was doing, she obviously was tired but other than that I could not tell. Her face was a mix of different emotions, while she had a smile her eyebrows showed that she was concerned and her eyes showed sadness. I feel bad, it is because of me that she is feeling like this right now, she is worried about me while I am worrying about her.

Although, some of that worry might be about confronting her father after all of this. She did run away and, while she did, her father threatened to burn down every house that belonged to a worker in order to find her. Now that I think of it, I really hope that my father is okay. He started a huge fight along with some of the other workers so that I could run of and look for Perdita.

Another thing I worry about is what the others are going to say when they see me coming back with Perdita, looking all banged up. If I told them that I fought a monster they will not believe me. However, that problem is solved. When they see the dark, circular object with a weak taint of red, that is hanging by my waist.

It is proof that whatever I am saying is true, and I might be able to use it in order to expose Perdita's father for all the things that he has done.

My line of thought was then broken by Perdita.

"Hey Spirit." She said quietly.

"Yeah?" I simply responded.

"Can we stop and talk for a second?" She asked, and I looked at her for two seconds before nodding.

We both sat down next to each other at a nearby log. She then took a deep breath before looking at me and asking.

"What happened to you during the battle?"

"What do you mean?" I responded. I think I knew what she meant, but still.

"I mean that glow that radiated from you." She said with an expression that showed confusion.

Now I knew what she was talking about, and it's a relief.

"You saw that too? I thought I was going crazy from all the blood loss." I said with a look that showed just as much confusion as her.

"Hey, even if you had lost a lot of blood it doesn't mean you can just start glowing red out of nowhere." She said like a teacher correcting a student.

"Well, my vision was turned completely red. So even though I could tell that light was coming out of my body, it was really hard to tell apart from the normal sunlight that was colored red thanks to my eyes going crazy." I said, like a student who desperately tried to explain himself.

"Okay, I can understand that, but still. Even if you couldn't tell what was red or not it doesn't explain the fact that, after you threw your punch, you got launched backwards." She then said to continue.

I was still confused of what that was. It was not like anything that I had ever seen before. Was this really, but no…

"Perhaps it's some type of magic" Perdita said to break my line of thought.

"Huh?" I responded, unable to fully comprehend what she meant.

"During my study I read about magic. It was said that magical abilities didn't appear, or rather, manifest until you were at a certain age. It also said that certain abilities didn't manifest until the user reached a certain requirement, like strength, intelligence or technique." She said, before pausing for breath and then continuing with.

"It also said that users might develop their own unique ability and sometimes they might inherit their ability from their parents. They can also learn certain techniques that's common for their race or family. But it's not rare that more than one person has a certain ability. However, the book that I read it in isn't so trustworthy. After all, nobody has seen or even heard a rumor of someone who can use magic, therefore we cannot be sure if what the book says is true and magic really does exist." She said to finish her long and detailed explanation.

Magic. I thought that every demon had darkness magic and every divine had light magic. But according to Perdita those things might just be that they have techniques that made it look like they all had the same ability. But she did also say that it was common for people to have a similar, if not the same, type of magic.

"I think it's now safe to assume that magic really does exist. Considering what has happened." I said. But just as I said it I got a sceptical look on my face. Perdita must have noticed it and asked.

"What's wrong?"

I took a long and deep breath and then said.

"If magic exists. Then does that mean that demons and angels exist too?" I said, with a clear voice. Perdita was shocked, as she did not respond with anything but a weird look. So I continued with.

"Think about it. All tales about demons and divine are all connected to magic somehow. It's even said that they have a magical ability that's exclusive to their races." I said with the same voice.

Perdita still did not respond, so I took her silence as an agreement to what I said.

Then, afterwards, the silence was broken by her asking.

"What should we name your ability?"

"Huh?" I responded in confusion once again. She wanted to name my ability?

"Yeah, in the tales every great warrior has an ability with a special name. We should name yours." She said.

"Like what? Red Fury?" I asked. Perdita got a grin that showed annoyance and said.

"No, that just sounds stupid."

"Well it makes sense. During the entire experience I was super angry and furious." I said with a voice to match Perdita's.

"Well, in that case why don't we call it something like… Vindicta." She said with a whisper.

"Vin- What?" I asked.

"Vindicta. It's ancient language that was practised so long ago that we don't even remember what it was called. On top of that, we can't speak it properly for it's grammar has been lost along with what we assume to be over seventy percent of all the words." She said, once again going full teacher mode.

"Anyway. The word 'Vindicta' represents our word for 'vengeance'." She said.

*Vindicta... Vengeance.*

My mind was racing all kinds of thoughts right now. Naming my ability 'vengeance' really makes sense after all. It does represent anger and rage in a way. On top of that, my ability didn't kick in until I was close to death and really angry. So much so that I wanted to take vengeance.

"I like it. Vindicta it is." I said, with a proud voice, and we both laughed.

But after a while her face was broken down into another worry. She asked.

"What are we going to do once we get back? I mean how are we going to explain your injuries, and..." She stopped for a second and then continued.

"And what are we going to do about my father? I don't want to go back with him Spirit. If I do I'll lose you forever." She said almost crying while looking up at me.

"Don't worry. We brought the monster's head remember, they'll believe me when I say that we had to fight it." I stopped for a second and then continued.

"Don't worry, you won't ever lose me and I won't ever lose you. I'll make sure that bastard can't lay a single finger on you. Even if you do have to go with him I will come and save you someday, I promise… Besides, I have my magical ability 'Vindicta', he can't stop me even if he tries." I said while looking at Perdita and smiling. She smiled back and we stood still for a while, holding eachothers hands.

Her hand felt so warm and was so smooth and beautiful. It felt like a crime for me to hold it with my large, rough and surprisingly dirty hand.

"We fought that monster? Last time I checked you were the only one doing anything." She said and broke the silence that we had.

"Well that's not entirely true, you help-" I was cut off by my own really rough coughing. It was so bad that I lent forward a bit, it almost felt like I was going to spit up my internal organs. In that moment Perdita placed both her hands on my shoulders, looked at me with a concerned look and said.

"Spirit, are you okay" To which I responded.

"Yeah I'm fine, don't worry" Then coughed some more.

For a while she was silent, but I could tell that she was really concerned. I could hear her breathing, and after a while she took a deep one and said.

"Okay, let's head back. The faster that you can get help the better." She said, while trying to help me up again, and placed my right hand over her shoulders again.

"Yeah, you got a point." I simply said, going along with what she was doing, as we started walking back to town again.

. . .

The rest of the way back to town went surprisingly smoothly, even with all of my injuries.

However, when we got back to my house I noticed that my father along with the rest of the other workers were still there, sitting on the ground as they were talking. It appears that the old man was finally gone, but I did not get the chance to think of anything else before I could hear a voice approaching me and yelling.

"Son!...Son, are you alright? What the hell happened to you?" It was father with a concerned look, he looked at me and my broken body before I said.

"I'm fine father, I just got in a fight with a monster in an attempt to save Perdita." I said, as smoothly as I possibly could with these injuries.

"Oh that's right. I take it that you are Perdita then?" He said, as he looked at her.

"Yes" Perdita answered.

"Anyway. Son, you said something about a monster. What do you exactly mean by that?" Father said, changing back the subject. I noticed that some of father's friends started jogging towards us. I reached to my waist, behind my back with my left hand, and pulled fourth the object that I had brought and said.

"This is what I mean. This thing was wandering around in the forest like nothing, until it started to chase me and Perdita to a mountain side. There I managed to kill it, but as you see I got really injured doing so."

Everyone was quiet and stared at the head of the beast. They then looked at eachother and started whispering. After a while father turned to his friends and said.

"We need to get a hunting team ready now! Tell them to look around in the area for any monster-like creatures and, if they do, they either have to kill it or make sure to track it so that we can hunt it down later."

The men looked at father and responded with

"Yes sir!" Before they took off. Father then turned back to us and said.

"Come on you two, we need to get inside so that I can fix your wounds. Perdita you can stay with us as long as you want. Spirit after I'm done with you I'm going back to the lake that we went fishing in the other day in order to investigate something. You need to stay here and rest so that those wounds can heal properly." With his hands on our shoulders, and we both at the same time responded by saying.

"Okay"

After father had finished with bandaging me, he placed me in my bed so that I could rest. Next to me sat Perdita on the edge of the bed, looking down at me with a smile. I smiled back and after a while, without saying anything, we interlocked our fingers and held hands. My recovery period will be long, however I am sure that with Perdita by my side I will get better much faster.

# *Interlude III*

I can not wrap my head around it at all. A monster in the forest, it sounds like a fairy tale but it is true. There are these behemoths roaming around. But based on what Spirit showed me earlier it just seems that a normal bear has gotten infected with something really strange and transformed into a monster. Not only that, but Spirit actually managed to kill that damn thing all on his own.

*Son, what happened to you?*

Was the only thought that I had while I wandered towards the so called 'Lake of behemoths', searching for answers to all of my questions.

Once I reached the lake I took a look around to make sure that the only ones who were listening were trees, boulders and rabbits.

After I was sure that I was alone I stepped forward towards the water and dipped my hands into it. The feeling was not that of a normal lake, for this one gave you a sense of nothing but a desire for chaos and a sensation that spread all around the arms like a fire.

There was nothing different from before. This lake was only altered for one purpose, and that was to make sure that the food that the townspeople consumed was infested with powers of chaos and destruction. To much exposure or consumption of this power would slowly but certainly turn all the normal humans into demons, beings of darkness. Or, if a demon were to be exposed to this, his powers would amplify greatly.

That was my original goal with poisoning the lake, the large fish was nothing but an unexpected side effect.

However, I did not even imagine that the animals other than the fish would grow large as well. It was an interesting result but it is not what I wanted. My son, he was going to grow strong from this. But instead it has damaged him and caused a nuisance for the both of us. This lake has failed its purpose, and I will now have to search for another option to reach my desired results.

But there is one thing that I still do not understand. How did Spirit even manage to defeat that beast if he has not been affected by the power?

Could it be that he still managed to defeat it? No that can not be it. If that was possible I would not be here doing this. So how? How did he, through all the pain from broken bones, bruises and the rage of battle, manage to def-

I stopped myself for a second, looked down at the water again as I came to my realization.

*The rage. Of course... Hehehe*

So my experiment was not to waste after all. He showed different results, such that I would not even dare to imagine. He did not become the being that I wanted. He did me one better and turned, no, awoke as a being with much more strength than I desired. Maybe even more strength that I had at this moment. A perfect creature, as powerful as a god, as ruthless as a beast and still he looks exactly like a normal human.

This lake. In a way it has now atoned for its own mistakes. Instead of altering all the humans it altered all the animals, thus creating monsters that then went and awoke my son from his eternal slumber. Now when the time comes he will be strong enough to stand up and rule, so that he one day can inherit my throne.

The divine. They better watch their backs, because now the monster that will bring their demise has arrived. He will burn every house, slaughter and enslave every living person and he will devour the Divine King's very soul.

As he looks at his brethren, his fellow demons with pride and glory, they will roar and cheer as the new Demon Emperor makes history of the divine race. It is destiny, whether they like it or not that day will come.

You may now start counting the days. For the day us demons, me, my son and the rest of our brethren stop. That is the day that we have forgotten to continue, and thus the divine will be erased from all existence. So please count your days. You will never know if someone, like us, decides to come and take them from you.

# <u>2</u>

"Come on! We have to move it's not safe here" I yelled with all my might as I tried to lift my fellow worker friend Joe, out of a pile of rubble and up to his feet with my blood soaked hands.

"I can't, my legs. I can't feel my legs!" Joe yelled back with stress and panic in his eyes as he tried to move his legs. I tried to help him even further but before I could do anything else he fell down onto his back and and blacked out.

After several attempts to wake him up I put my ear to his chest, and my finger to his throat. There was nothing, not a single thud could be heard. It was hard for me to accept, but Joe was now dead.

How did this even happen? The houses are on fire, the people are screaming as they are dying and some are being taken away. I was on my knees as I looked up at the night sky. It was covered in a thick sheath of smoke so that the only light that was provided was from flames on the scorched foundations that used to be houses.

*Why? What did we do to deserve this?*

Was the only thing that I could think of while I was just sitting there frozen in place. It had been three days since I fully recovered, Perdita had stayed with me and father still.

*Father... Perdita*

A new thought raced in my mind. I need to find them now. I got up to my feet once more and took off running towards the noble's district. Perdita was most likely there due to them having the best defence in crises, however I doubt that even their defence will last against this.

Whatever was attacking us was neither monsters or bandits. These were soldiers that would stop at nothing to reach their goal, including showing no mercy even for defenceless townspeople like us.

As I ran past all the burning structures I could hear a familiar voice call my name.

"Spirit!" He yelled and as I turned around I yelled back with tears in my eyes.

"Father! Fath-" I could not finish. For as soon as I tried to say it a loud noise, resembling that of a medium explosion, was heard from my right. My smile faded away completely as I stopped on my heels and witnessed as my father tumbled down to the left.

My mind went blank, after he started falling everything went in slow motion and all the noise around me was completely erased.

Father fell down to the ground with his mouth open in the shape that it would be taking during a scream of pain, but I could not hear it. As he crashed into the ground everything turned back to normal and I ran through all the mud on the ground until I fell down to my knees next to father.

I started crying my eyes out, as I tried to speak.

"F-f-father" He looked up at me with blood coming out of his mouth and, with the last strength that he had, said.

"S-son. It's okay. My t-time has come now."

"No father, you can't leave me now I need you. There's so much more that I haven't learned from you." I said with eyes still pouring out tears and my voice trembling.

"No son. You have learnt so much... Y-You'll be fine..." He stopped for a second and I could not say anything, my throat and vocal chords were completely numb. He then grabbed on to my right shoulder and said.

"Son, t-there's something that you should know. No, that you need to know. You a-are not a human and neither am I... I-I was born a demon a-and so were you. It is why y-you could defeat the beast the other day. Your powers have now been awakened, and you need to master them."

He then paused for breath, and I was in complete shock.

*I'm not h-human? I'm a demon?* What father said made no sense, how could I have been a demon for my entire life if I only just felt it. My line of thought was canceled when father muttered out his last words.

"Son I am so proud of you..." He said as his last breath left his throat. I could not comprehend it, I started crying and screaming. He was gone and he was not coming back.

*Why? Why is this happening to us? Why did they come here to destroy our town and kill my father? Why?!*

Were the only thoughts that went through my head before everything went in slow motion again, and all noises were being dulled out.

I could not comprehend anything. As I closed my tearful eyes I could hear a dulled voice screaming from behind me.

"-p-r-t"

 I opened my eyes again and the dull effect vanished, in that moment I could hear the voice calling me.

"Spirit!!!" It was a high pitched voice that I could recognize anywhere. It was Perdita.

As I turned around to face her I could see her face that was dirty from all the smoke and mud. She was terrified, pointed towards the direction that the original shots had come from, and yelled.

"Look out!!!" I looked over in that direction and saw it. There were five men, no, soldiers lifting up their rifles and pointing them at me. I tried to move, but I just could not. My legs, they just would not move.

As they took aim and where ready to fire I once again closed my eyes and tried to wait until it was over. The sounds of the gunfire explosions were once again dulled, and I awaited my end. But once the bullets collided I did not feel anything. The only thing that I felt was something warm but wet splashing onto me.

As I opened my eyes I was placed in another shock. A figure was standing in front of me and had taken all the bullets that were meant for me, and nobody else. It took me awhile, but I realized who this person was. It was Perdita.

After the wave of bullets had hit her she fell down to the ground where I was sitting, and I caught her. I held her in my arms as I looked her in the eyes.

She was forming some small tears through a smile, as she with her last breath said.

"T-thank you. G-goodbye." I was completely still as her life poured out of her body. I could feel something cold and wet flow down my cheeks as I was screaming in pain without any stop.

*Why? Why are you taking everything that I hold dear away from me? Tell me, WHY?!?!?!*

I looked over at the men with a hateful stare. They were laughing, they were laughing at my misery.

These people, the ones that lived in this town only tried to find their place in the world, and they, they were laughing at their dead bodies.

Before I knew it I was standing in my feet again. The next thing I did was to leap onto the men that stood only ten meters away from me.

It was to no avail as the man standing in the very front of the group knocked me back three meters so that I crashed into the ground. Even more laughter grew from the group. This only infuriated me. As I tried to stand up again I saw on my left side. There was a sickle, left by a farmer who ran for his life to no avail.

Completely furious from that thought I grabbed the sickle with my right hand and heard the men laughing and mocking me for it.

In that moment I felt it again, the overflow of energy and rage. My vision started to turn red as I started growling and feeling like my body was turing lighter and stronger by the second. I have felt this power before, back when I killed the beast.

It was my magical ability 'Vindicta'. Named by no other than the girl who sacrificed her own life for my sake. Only this time it was different, it was more intense than before, It was... Stronger.

I pointed at the men, sickle in hand and said.

"You...You will pay for that...You will pay... For everything!!" Next thing I did was leap at the men again and, as my charged up attack with the sickle connected, everything went completely black.

I lost control of myself and now I could not do anything to stop it. All I could do now was stare into this void and wait, until my bloodlust had been clenched.

# *3*

As I ripped my sickle out of the man's throat, I felt a splash of warm and red liquid over my face. I let out a heavy breath, and then let go of his corpse.

His body fell onto the ground without a sound, and I looked around to see what I had created with my might and weapon in hand.

There was ashes on empty foundations, signaling that there used to be a structure in these set locations. The soil in the ground was burnt and drenched in blood, it would never bear life ever again. On the ground were piles and shredded pieces of what used to be living, innocent humans, but they all laid dead on the ground like a trophy to my single-handed mass slaughter.

I looked upwards towards the sky, closed my eyes and took a deep breath. This was my doing, now I will take a moment to enjoy the results and let them soak in.

I then opened my eyes as I exhaled with a broad smile across my face. But then I heard a voice. It seemed to be coming from just below me.

"W-why?" It said like a whisper. That voice, it was familiar. I turned around and then looked below myself. At that moment I could hear two voices instead, the other belonging to a girl.

When my eyes finally found the sources of the voices my body went completely tense and my heart started beating so much that I thought that it was going to explode right out of my chest.

It cannot be true, the two people who were trying to whisper to me were no other than father and Perdita. I looked in their half opened eyes on their blood soaked and pale faces. As they with almost all their remaining strength said.

"Why Spirit? Why did you murder us?" My heart started racing like crazy, if it went on any longer I could get a heart attack. I could feel the sweat flowing down my face and I started screaming.

"NO! I-I didn't!! I- I'm so sorry. No! No! NOOOOO!!!!!" I screamed until I rocked forwards, covered in sweat inside of something that looked like a giant box, with other strangers sitting next to me.

*It was just a dream?* I thought as I looked around and raised my hands to dry my face from all the sweat. But I soon realized that it was not possible. For my hands were tied together and, not only that, they were also connected to my loosely tied feet with a chain.

*What is going on? Where am I? What happened?*

The first thing I remember was being in town when it burned down, and in the next moment I was here.

I looked around the giant box and noticed a window just across from me. I could see clouds and trees passing by through the really small window, and if I listened really carefully I could hear something that was similar to the sound made once stepping onto gravel.

*We are moving, but where are we being taken?*

Before I could answer that, the man who sat next to me said.

"Oh, you're awake, are you alright?" He asked with a soft voice. I looked at the man and noticed something. He was not human. His skin color was bright orange, he had red goat horns on his head and his face and bare arms were covered in pitch-black hairs. It took me a while, but I finally figured out what he was.

"Yeah I'm fine... You're a demon, aren't you?" I said casually while leaning against the wall to my right.

"Yeah I am, we all are. Except for you it may appear." He answered. His answer got me curious so I took a look around, and he was right. Everybody in this carriage looked inhuman in some bizarre way.

"Well that's not true. I'm a demon as well, although I didn't know it until almost a day ago, I think." I said, because it was true. I am indeed a demon, according to what father said, and right now the fact that I am a demon is the only explanation to the powers that I possess for some reason.

The goat-demon looked at me with a completely shocked expression, and then said.

"Wait, you're a demon? But you look just like a human. That's strange, I have never seen a demon

look like a human since their birth and, on top of that, not knowing that they are one." He said, and then continued by asking.

"Hey kid, what's your name?" I was a bit shocked by that question, but I looked up at him and answered.

"It's Spirit... Nihilanth 'N' Spirit. I'm from what I guess you could call the land that's in between the The Divine and The Demons." The demon, once again, looked shocked as he said.

"You're from the planet Exile?... I'm so sorry that you had to be born and raised in the middle of a warzone... Anyway, my name is Dim' jordano... Sal 'ta' ir Dim' jordano."

Dim' jordano, planet Exile. His name was unusual for sure but I have never heard somebody call my birthplace "Exile", and on top of that he referred to it as planet. What does he mean. Well, now that I think about it, no one ever talked about the planet or anything happening in the outside world unless it concerned us directly.

That was probably why we were not able to defend ourselves against the attack. My line of thought was once again broken by Dim' jordano.

"What are you doing here? You're nothing but a ten year old kid, so what does The Divine want with you?" He asked, and I was confused for a bit. What happened during the attack that made me end up here? I remember father and Perdita dying, and then I recall some soldiers laughing at my misery and then I-

I stopped thinking for a second. I did it, I slaughtered those soldiers. But if I am here then that means that they were Divine soldiers, and so were the rest of the people attacking my home. I took a deep breath, looked at Dim' jordano, and answered the question.

"I-I killed a group of Divine soldiers."

He looked at me with a confused expression and asked.

"What?"

"I killed some Divine soldiers. My town was being attacked and they burned down all the houses, killed and enslaved the population... And killed my father and best friend in front of my eyes. This enraged me, so I charged at the soldiers that were responsible, and then I blacked out. I can't recall what happened exactly, but I just had a nightmare of me murdering a group of men. If I am here then it can only mean that the ones who attacked and destroyed my town were no other than The Divine." As I said that I noticed that every demon inside the carriage were looking at me. Just like Dim' jordano, they were shocked out of their lives.

"Y-You killed a group of Divine soldiers alone? What kind of demon are you?... To hell with the Divine, how dare they raid an innocent town like that." He said, with both a shocked and angry expression.

All the other demons started chatting with each other about what they just heard. But those chats turned short because the cart just suddenly stopped moving.

"End of the line." I said, with a tired and exhausted voice.

"Yeah, I guess so. I'm sorry that this has to be your fate." He responded with a look that was a combination of sorrow and terror. I could not blame him, I felt the same. I did not know what was going to happen, and if I ever was going to enjoy my freedom again.

The door to the carriage was opened by a man wearing armor, and he shouted.

"Alright get out and move towards the platform, now!!!" As soon as the door was open.

I did not think twice. I got out, with Dim' jordano behind, me and walked up to the platform that they were referring to. It was made out of wood and stood high up on four legs.

When I turned to my left I noticed a crowd of people looking at me and the other demons, shouting and cursing us. It was so loud, and someone threw a can at my left shoulder once I reached the wooden stairs to the platform. The guards did not seem to care as they shouted that I should hurry up, and so I did.

Once I got up to the platform, the guard that opened the door earlier pushed me down to my knees then walked left to do the same to the others. I gazed off into that direction and saw Dim' jordano's sorry face again, and whispered.

"I'm sorry..." Really quietly so that the guards would not notice. He looked back at me, and nodded once. We already knew what was coming and made our last thoughts about something that we held dear, even if it was gone.

"Alright listen up everyone. These people are all demons. They are impure creatures that have committed crimes against The Divine King." A man with blue hair, who wore shining silver armor, a large blue cloak and a curved sword at his hip said. I assumed that man was the leader of these soldiers. But, before I got the chance to think about it, he walked up to me and, with a loud voice, asked.

"Tell me demon, do you have any last words?!"

I could hear the crowd roar in anger as they thought that I did not deserve the liberty of last words.

However, I just ignored them, for I was stuck in a long line of thought.

*My last words? What would they be? What do I want these people, The Divine, the bastards that took my home and life from me, to remember after I die here.*

I thought about it for a while, and then decided.

"Yeah, I have a few actually." I said, as I looked left to meet with Dim' jordano's eyes.

"Us demons, won't stop coming at you. No matter how many times you burn, slice and torture us, we will still come back." I stopped for breath and looked left and saw Dim' jordano, he wore a shocked expression.

"We won't stop until you all are gone... One day, one beautiful day, we will destroy every last trace of you all... You can't stop us, you know why?! Because the Hellfire has been ignited by none other than yourselves, and it will burn you all to ashes!!!." I yelled with all my might. I turned to my left, and saw that Dim' jordano and the rest of the demons were all roaring and cheering. They all understood what I meant and they felt it as they cheered in agreement.

I then turned to my right, and saw a man winding up a swing with a sword in both of his hand. He then finished winding, and swung down at my neck.

For a split second I could hear Dim' jordano screaming my name, as I felt the cold steel sinking into me. Then, suddenly, the crowd and noises all went away, as everything went completely black with no noise or anything.

. . .

I could not tell if my eyes were open or not, everything was pitch black. I could not even tell which way I was facing.

I already know what happend. The sword was swung onto my neck, and thus ended my life.

I do not know where you go after you die. But I, like my father, I believed that there was an afterlife for everybody, regardless of what you might have been convicted for in life.

So when I died. I half heartedly expected to be reunited with Perdita and my father, but that did not happen. I was stuck in one massive, and dark, spot.

*I do not understand this. If I am indeed dead, why am I still capable of thinking, and why am I in this void of all things.* I thought as I kept staring.

I kept looking around everywhere, and when I looked in the direction that I thought was forward, I noticed a small point of light in the far distance. I started to glare at it even more and noticed that it slowly, but certainly, grew larger and turned red. The light just grew larger and larger, until it totally engulfed me and turned my field of view pure red.

After a few seconds the light died out, and I noticed something strange. I was not in the void anymore, I was in some sort of large room with dark red pillars supporting the roof. The walls were, like the pillars and every other structure inside this room, colored dark red. But they also had engravings of humanoid creatures battling each other with all kinds of weapons. The floors and ledges were decorated with bright red carpets and hanging curtains.

I was wondering for a second where I was, and how I got here, but before I could think of an answer I heard a voice from across the room.

"What's this? Someone is in my throne room?" He indirectly answered my question. I was in some sort of throne room. It made sense when you thought about it. Across the room from where I was standing, was a large throne facing away from me. It would appear that the man talking was sitting in it.

"Oh. I see. You're him, aren't you? You're here a bit too early wouldn't you say my child? Ah well, it doesn't matter now." He said as he reached out his right hand to the right so that it was visible to me. I was a good twenty meters away from the throne, so observing what his hand looked like would be difficult. The only thing that I could tell for sure was that he appeared to have long claws for fingernails.

"Well, I guess I can introduce myself." He said as he started standing up and, once he stood up and started walking towards me, continued.

"I am The Demon Emperor, also known as Ordi'nah. I rule the demon realm, my child. Right now we are standing in my palace, inside the capital of the demon realm."

*Wait. Am I right now face to face with The Demon Emperor himself? How the hell did I end up here?*

Were my only thoughts, but before I could ask any questions he said.

"I'm sure that you are confused. You must have a lot of questions. But don't worry, one day they will all be answered. Just not today."

*He would not answer my questions? Why, there is so much I don't understand.* Was what I thought, but before I could say it, or anything at all since I arrived here, he said.

"Well, I think it's time for you to go back now. Stay out of trouble." He said.

*What do you mean by tha-*

My thought was cut off by me being sucked into a small, black vortex that twisted my perception of reality. For a while it was nauseating, but then it felt

strange. Like I was getting my sense of feeling back into my body. But then everything went black again.

I opened my eyes, and blinked many times until my vision came back fully. I was on my knees and my hands were tied together. I took a good look around and noticed all the demons, including Dim' jordano, to my left, and in front of me was the crowd of people still screaming and cursing us. I was back here, did I not die?

I looked left to try and make eye contact with Dim' jordano. Once we did he went pale and screamed.

"Spirit?! What the hell, you're still alive?" As he screamed that, the other demons, guards and people in the crowd all went pale at the same time when they caught the glimpse of me, still alive.

The captain of the guards went from pale to red, as he yelled.

"You damn idiots!!! Can't you even kill a ten year old demon properly?" To the guards that were in charge of this execution. They both started sweating and, with panic, apologised to their captain. This seemed to make the captain even angrier, and he yelled.

"Do it properly this time!!! Kill him and then keep slicing and cutting him up afterwards!!!"

He then started breathing really heavily. Screaming like that took all of his remaining breath.

The guards followed his orders. They wound up their swings and, once they let go, I was met with a familiar feeling of cold steel.

Everything went pitch-black again. But this time the crimson glow surrounded me and I could feel how something was growing inside of me. It was something that I was all too familiar with. A raging fire that spread throughout my entire body, only this time it lasted way longer and while it did, it grew in both strength and rage.

I woke up from being cut down again, and noticed the men still cutting at me. At that moment the fire got worse, and my vision turned crimson red, as I let out a loud and menacing

*RRRAAAAGGHHHH!!!!*

Then everything went black again. But this time it was because of my bloodlust, not my supposed death.

# 4

I opened my eyes and found myself sitting in an armchair with my arms on both the resters. My left hand was empty, but my right hand was holding on to a bloody sickle. When my vision came back fully I took a good look around, and noticed that I was inside some sort of old cabin. The walls were made out of wood, but they were really torn and looked like they were going to break into pieces at any moment. I also noticed a table made from the same material as the walls, with two backpacks on top of it.

*What happened and how did I end up here?* I asked myself. But then I heard some footsteps coming towards me. I looked in that direction and saw a demon with orange skin, red goat horns and black hairs over his body.

"Dim' jordano?" I asked. He stopped right in front of me, crouched, and said.

"Good, you're awake. Are you alright?" He asked as he put his hand on my shoulder.

"Yeah, I think so. What happened?" I said with a tired look on my face.

"Well, the execution was interrupted by your... Whatever it is that you did. I, along with the others, managed to escape in all the chaos that it caused. So I carried you on my back to a carriage that we, along with the other demons, took to a place that we could find transportation to Planet Exile. After that I carried you to this abandoned cabin, while the others kept traveling so that they could get back to the demon realm." He said, as he brushed his eyebrows.

"Why do you wanna get back to The Demon realm so badly?" I asked, keeping my tired look.

He looked at me, with a real face, and said.

"Because it's our home. We are soldiers, Spirit. We don't get to spend much time home because we are expected to die for the sake of the empire." He said, while putting his other hand on my other shoulder. He then stood up, helped me to my feet, and continued by saying.

"Anyway, we need to get whatever we can for the trip. Once we get to the demon realm let me do the talking, because it's probably going to take a lot to convince them that you are a demon. But once we get through you can stay with me for as long as you like. One day, if you want to join our military, I'll pass a letter of recommendation to the commander." As he said that I could not help but get a weird feeling. He wanted me to come with him to the demon realm, but I am not sure if I truly belong there. Because, through my blackout, I have faint memories about what I did.

"The other demons didn't make it. I killed them, right?" I said, as I looked over at Dim' jordano. He had an expression that showed what I uttered was true.

"Then I can't come to the demon realm. I'll stay here until I find out who I truly am." I said, as I looked into the ground. Dim' jordano had a sad expression on his face.

He probably understood how I felt. My father and best friend were killed in front of me and, on top of that, I myself killed half a dozen of demons, my own kind. I cannot go to the demon realm yet.

"Alright then, if that is how you feel then I won't stop you. But promise me one thing. When you do decide to come to the demon realm, you will find me. I will help you." He said as he put his hand on my shoulder once again.

"Thank you Dim' jordano"

"Oh, please call me Dim' jo. All my friends call me that. And you, Spirit, are certainly my friend." I looked up at him after he said that. He was smiling, my friend. A warm feeling filled my heart, and I smiled too.


. . .


After we finished packing everything up, Dim' jo and I started walking. Once we got to a point where the road split in two we stopped, and looked at eachother.

"Well, I guess this is it then." I said.

"Yeah, I guess it is... Tell me, what are you going to do?" Dim'jo asked. I took a while to consider. Then I looked at the sickle that I held in my right hand still, and said.

"I'm going to master the power within me and, in that process, find out who I am. But in order to do that I'll have to become something else." I said while looking Dim' jo straight in the eyes with a serious look. He then blinked and asked.

"What is it that you will become?" He asked.

I tightened my grip around the sickle in my hand, took a deep breath, and said.

"From this day forward. I'm Raze. The Crimson Reaper, Raze." I said, with a proud voice.

"Alright. Then once I get back the demon realm I will pass a message to the commander. Saying that a powerful demon called 'The Crimson Reaper, Raze' will be a great ally to have. I will tell him how 'The Reaper' saved my life and is powerful enough to single handedly defeat an entire squad of medium ranking Divine soldiers, and cheat death more than once." He said with a proud voice, to which I just nodded.

We both looked at eachother, waved goodbye, and then walked down our own separate paths. From now on I was free, I can do whatever I want. But right now the only thing that I want to do is fight, so that I can grow stronger.

This is not how I imagined my freedom. I am alone, and I am confused.

I looked to my left and saw a translucent figure of a girl wearing a blue dress with white sleeves. She had brown hair, brown eyes and a bright skin tone. It was Perdita, I had to sacrifice her for my freedom.

I closed my eyes for a moment, and when I opened them she was gone without a trace.

In that moment I just exhaled, and then I looked forward, towards the village in the far distance at the end of my road.

A feeling of nostalgia entered my mind thanks to the view, but I pushed it away and proceeded forward towards the village so that I could start reaching my new goal.

*The world will know my name, they will know my wrath, my power and pain. They will regret making an enemy of me.*

# Interlude IV

"Oh man this wine sure is something. I can't believe this taste." I said, before I took another sip of my golden drink.

"Oh, and this beer is just awesome. But you know what's even better? When you combine it with some Elven wine." I said as I, with a broad smile, poured the wine into my beer glas, and then took a sip.

"Hmm. This is amazing! Wouldn't you agree 'boss'." I said as I stepped over a bloody corpse on the floor, and then passed the five others lying on the nearby bar-tables.

The once beautiful bar now looked like a morgue because of what had happened five minutes ago. I had simply walked into the bar because I had heard that the guy I was hunting was here, his men kept calling him 'boss' so I did that as well. But when the bartender, and the six men that 'boss' had with him, started pointing weapons and attacking me...
Things got ugly, in a very bloody way, very fast.

As I got closer to the man called "boss" his face just went paler and paler with each footstep. Until I stopped and noticed something odd...

*How mischievous of you, 'boss'*

I thought as I smiled, took another footstep, and continued forward. But then I saw his hand swinging forward, holding on to a pistol. I just managed to stop as I heard the.

*Phff!!*

From the gunshot. I looked down at my chest and saw red liquid flowing out of a small round hole. I placed my drink on a table, and then I fell down to my knees.

"Yes, it surely is one of the most amazing things in the world. Savour the taste, it will be your last. Now people will know not to mess with me and my metal business. Hahaha!" 'Boss' said with a grin on his face, and a laughter.

He just looks ridiculous. A short fat man, with a thick black mustache and bald head, wearing a fine suit. A stereotypical maffia.

While he was enjoying himself I wrapped my left hand around his neck and stood up, lifting the fat dwarf up in the air. His expression went from jolly to an expression that showed all hope has been crushed.

I looked down and heard the weak sound of a metallic object falling to the ground, as my wound pushed the bullet out and then closed together, healing perfectly. I then looked back at boss and said.

"Oh, I will enjoy it. But now people will know to fear me instead, and so I will use that as my weapon in the future."

'Boss' looked at me, his expression the same and with a tembeling voice asked.

"What kind of monster are you? You're just sixteen years ol-" He could not continue his words over the sickle blade inside his throat. All he could do now was choke and make weird noises.

"I'm no monster." I said before I, with all my might, ripped the sickle to the right, gutting up the man's throat. As the fat-man was, slowly but certainly, dying by choking on his own blood, due to his throat being shredded to pieces, I ended my monologue.

"I'm a Demon... I am 'The Crimson Reaper, Raze' "

# ***Afterword***

Hey there, Abraham "Sylander" Jidah here. Thank you for reading Reaper's origins 1 Hellfire: Ignited. This novel took a while to make if you start from the point that the idea first came to my mind. Back then it was just me and my friend creating our own characters and later building up bigger stories than I thought.

This novel is the origin of my character, Nihilanth 'N' Spirit - or Crimson Reaper, Raze if you prefer. When I created him for the first time I just thought that it would be cool to have a half-human, half-demon wielding a scythe. Then when my friend and I decided that we could take these stories and write them down into novels and manga I got fired up.

I was the only one who actually wrote this book, but I had discussions with friend about the different parts in the story, like how Spirit's ability should work.

When we made the original story, we realized that it would leave a lot of questions and holes, so we decided to start by creating the backstories of our characters so that when the story in these novels end, the original story that we first made would begin. Look forward to that if you liked this book.

Also there will be another book following this one. It will follow from where the last interlude ended. Where it has passed six years since his father and friend died. Raze will find himself in a situation were he will have to learn to cooperate with others and let them in to his now closed off heart. You could say that the next book will be centered around his family and relationships.

Anyway, soon enough my friend will release his own novel about his own character. It will just take a while for us to release new books for we will have to put up with studies at the same time. Also this is my first time ever making a book so please take it with a grain of salt. If you want you can send some feedback.

Before I end this I just want to say that when making most of the names in this book I just took random words and translated them to latin or greek. 'Perdita' for example means 'lost' in latin, 'Unum' means 'The one and only' in latin and 'To éna' means 'The one' in greek. The only names that weren't like this were, 'Warden' and 'Dim'jo'. 'Warden' was just random, but 'Dim'jo'. That one was when my friend spelled Daimyo wrong, and I just thought that it was too good to just pass by.

Anyway to end this I want to say thank you to all my friends for reading through my work and giving me advice, my friends whom I discussed the story with and my parents and other family members for supporting me with this.(Sorry for not telling you earlier dad.)

 I also want to give a special thanks to the illustrator Grigory Kornienko, with whom I seemed to share a telepathic connection, for the BEAUTIFUL drawings he made. There are so many wonderful details in every drawing, each one ends up telling a beautiful story of their own.

Thank you for reading. I'll see you in the next one.

- *Abraham "Sylander" Jidah (2020)*